MEET FREDDIE O'NEAL

". . . A UNIQUE AND ENGAGING CRIME FIGHTER . . . WHO LIKES CATS AND KENO AND WHO GAMBLES WITH HER OWN LIFE IN TANGLING WITH CRIME IN RENO."
—*Abilene Reporter-News*

LAY IT ON THE LINE, *nominated for a Shamus Award by the Private Eye Writers of America*: Freddie's got some legwork to do when an ex-chorus girl asks for her help investigating a case of fraud that turns into a case of murder . . .

"APPEALING CHARACTERS AND AN INTRIGUING PLOT . . . A WINNER."
—**Linda Grant, author of *Love nor Money***

SING A SONG OF DEATH: Vince Marina was the hottest lounge act in Lake Tahoe. Now he's gone to the big casino in the sky—and Freddie has to find out who *really* lowered the curtain on Vince . . .

"CATHERINE DAIN DELIVERS A FAST-PACED STORY WITH TOUCHES OF WRY HUMOR AND POIGNANCY . . . WONDERFUL CHARACTERS . . . WHAT MORE CAN A READER ASK FOR?"
—**Maxine O'Callaghan**

WALK A CROOKED MILE: Freddie thought her long-lost father was out of her life. But when she agrees to track him down at her mother's request, she digs up more than just family skeletons . . .

"FREDDIE O'NEAL IS A LATTER-DAY TRAVIS McGEE . . . A HELL OF A READ."
—**David Hagberg, award-winning author of *Countdown* and *Crossfire***

MORE MYSTERIES FROM THE
BERKLEY PUBLISHING GROUP . . .

Walk a Crooked Mile

CATHERINE DAIN

JOVE BOOKS, NEW YORK

WALK A CROOKED MILE

A Jove Book / published by arrangement with
the author

PRINTING HISTORY
Jove edition / February 1994

ISBN: 0-515-11310-7

A JOVE BOOK®
Jove Books are published by The Berkley Publishing Group,
200 Madison Avenue, New York, New York 10016.
JOVE and the "J" design
are trademarks belonging to Jove Publications, Inc.

PRINTED IN THE UNITED STATES OF AMERICA

10 9 8 7 6 5 4 3 2 1

Chapter
1

CAMELS STINK WORSE than goats. They're ugly, they spit, and I have never heard of anyone waxing romantic about one, the way people do about horses sometimes, nor of anybody adopting a camel for a pet. The International Camel Races have been held in Virginia City longer than I've been alive, and not once did it occur to me to drive for an hour in the September heat to watch a bunch of good ol' boys with sobriquets du jour of Wild Bill, Wyatt, Doc Holiday, or what have you, get falling down drunk, and then try to get a mean-spirited camel to turn a corner and head for the finish line.

Until this year. When I found myself standing on the warped boardwalk in front of the Bucket o' Blood Saloon looking through the tourist horde for a middle-aged biker named Sam Courter. Because my mother had said this was as likely a place as any to find him.

Shit.

Mom had stopped by to see me about a month earlier, to my surprise, because she doesn't come down from Lake Tahoe often, and almost never without Al. This means our visits are limited to how long Al and I can stand to be in the same room, which is maybe half an hour. And she always calls first, to warn me. So I really didn't expect to find Mom on the porch, with Sundance, my orange tomcat, in her arms and nuzzling her cheek, when I answered the knock at the door.

"I need to talk to you," she said.

"Yeah, okay, I'll get my keys, and we can go someplace for coffee."

Letting Mom in always means losing the first ten minutes to a round of criticism of my housekeeping and my coffee. Not that either is above criticism. In fact, both are pretty bad. I just don't like hearing all that—again—from my mother.

"No. I want to talk in your office. This is business."

She had her spike heels firmly planted, and there was no way she was budging. I could have picked her up and carried her to the car—she's small enough—but I don't have the gall. I stepped out of the way and let her into the office.

I knew it was serious when she ignored the mess, except for clearing a couple of magazines off a folding chair so that she could sit. She dropped her bag—patchwork leather with a rose in red and green sequins—next to the chair, crossed her legs, and let Sundance settle down on her lap, petting him as he purred. She didn't even mind that he was kneading her black spandex bicycle pants. Mom has better legs at whatever-age-she-is than I have ever had in my life.

It didn't matter that she wasn't criticizing my office. Just having her there, I was doing it myself. There were papers askew on the desk, books askew on the shelves, and the only clear space was around the computer, which was on. Small businesses tend to founder on the rocky shoals of accounts receivable, and I was diligently sending out letters to some unfortunate souls whose need for service had been greater than their ability to pay. I try to watch out for that, I really do, but sometimes I misjudge, and then I hàve to collect.

One past-due account I was considering collecting with a baseball bat.

I sat down behind the desk and turned the screen low, not wanting to burn it out.

Mom had caught her reflection in the glass of my framed Union Pacific poster, pulled a brush out of her purse to untangle her long copper curls—a warmer shade than I had seen on her before—let the brush fall, and leaned forward.

"Freddie, I need help."

I was stunned. Mom never needed help with anything.

"What?"

"It's Al—"

I felt a surge of hope. Maybe she was finally leaving him.

"He's decided to run for the legislature," she finished.

"What does that have to do with me?"

I was unreasonably let down. I was also annoyed that my cat was sleeping on her lap. I got up and pulled Butch, my gray tomcat, from his spot on the second shelf of the bookcase. I knew he was there because my dictionary was on the floor. He screamed when I grabbed him, but calmed down when he realized he was going to be held and petted. I sat in the squeaky leather chair behind my desk. If Mom wanted business, we'd talk business.

"You know how nasty politics can get," she said, arranging the proper drape to her off-the-shoulder, cotton knit tunic, pale green with a silver bead design.

"A state legislature race? For a Lake Tahoe seat? Come on."

She glared at me.

"This is still Nevada. And Al would be running as an outsider. There's no telling what an insider—a tool of the tourist industry who wants unlimited development at the lake—might do. Dig into his past, looking for mud to sling. I don't want Al to be vulnerable."

"You don't want *you* to be vulnerable." She opened her mouth and shut it again. So I continued. "I'd bet a thousand dollars that not one of Al's closets has so much as a rat-sized skeleton in it. I have to say, though, that Al running as a slow-growth candidate is a shocker. Biting the hand that used to feed him, isn't he?"

"Al was a responsible developer, not like those greedy bastards who would dump sewage into the lake, destroying a national treasure to line their own pockets. Besides, he's retired, and we live there."

"Right. So what is it you want me to do?"

"I want you to find your father."

I was speechless.

"I'll pay you," Mom said, misinterpreting.

"Why?"

"Because I want you to think of this as a job, just like any other job, and I want you to devote some time to it without worrying about money."

"And my fee comes out of Al's campaign fund. But that isn't what I meant. Why do you want me to find—him?" I was going to say his name, but it wouldn't quite come out.

"I need him to do something for me."

I waited.

"I need him to sign the divorce papers," she said, pursing her burgundy lips, oblivious for the moment of the little lines the gesture deepened.

"After all these years? Wouldn't it be easier to have him declared dead?"

"No. And this isn't coming out of Al's campaign fund—Al doesn't know about it. Nobody knows that Danny didn't sign the papers."

"And you're afraid somebody's going to find out, and it will mess up your marriage to Al? You really think anyone would care?"

"Al would care," she snapped. "Al is a very conservative person, and it would hurt him deeply to think that there had been anything irregular about our marriage, or that people might think we were living in sin."

"Mom, if Tarzan and Jane were married in the eyes of God, so are you and Al. Anyway, Danny"—I barely skipped a beat as I said the word—"had been gone for almost a year when you got the divorce, and Al knew it. How could he have thought Danny signed the papers?"

"I lied."

I could never decide whether I admired or despised that in Mom, the way she accepted even her worst qualities if she thought they helped her survive.

"I told Al that it was a fortunate coincidence that Danny just happened to show up in Reno one night when I needed him to sign the papers. Traveling through on his way to nowhere. And, of course, I made him understand that it was better for everyone if he never tried to get in touch with us again."

"Of course." Of course she would come up with a story that put her in control. Danny hadn't abandoned her—she had told him not to come back. "And just how do you expect me to find him?"

"Well, I've thought about that. I tried to come up with someone he might have kept in touch with. Danny sent a postcard—the one that said he was gone for good—with a Las Vegas postmark. And he had one friend in Vegas, from the Marines, a man named Sam Courter."

"Have you tried the Las Vegas telephone directory?"

"Don't get snippy with me. Of course I have. One initial D. O'Neal, a Dan, and two Daniels. I called all four with no luck. No Sam Courter, either."

"Then how the hell do I find Sam Courter?"

"You might try the camel races."

I must have looked blank.

"The camel races," she said patiently, "in Virginia City. Danny went to the camel races every year because Sam would come up from Las Vegas for them. One of those male bonding things. I went to the races once, about ten years ago, and Sam was still there. He hadn't changed much—he had long hair, a leather jacket, and a Harley—and he was riding a camel sponsored by one of the local bordellos. If he isn't there this year, maybe someone would remember him and know where he is."

"Great, Mom, just great." I shook my head, belying the words. "Is there anything else helpful you can think of?"

"No, not yet. But I'm working on it. How much do you want for a retainer?"

I considered telling her it was on the house, but then I thought about my accounts receivable, and our relative financial situations.

"Just the thousand dollars I bet that it wasn't Al's past we were worried about."

She beamed at me as she rummaged for her checkbook.

"You remind me so much of Danny sometimes—the thousand-dollar bet was one of his lines, you know. 'If you want to know how a man really feels, ask him to back up his opinion with a thousand-dollar bet.' I'm sure you'll find him, dear."

This was the first time reminding her of Danny had ever been a compliment. I took the check.

"I'll be in touch," I told her.

Sundance complained as she eased him to the carpet and said good-bye. I didn't.

I sat there at my desk after she left, trying to think what I knew of my father. Not very much. He missed two years of my childhood when he was in Vietnam, moved in and out of the house for several stormy years after he got back, and was gone for good by the time I was fifteen.

I remembered a big man, with blond hair that sprang up wildly from his head, grew long on his neck, and turned red where his sideburns began. He wore western shirts with the cuffs rolled back, and his forearms were thick and covered with blond hair almost like fur. I remembered liking to touch his arm.

He was easy to walk with—not like Mom, I always felt horsey walking down the street with Mom. Walking with Danny, I felt as if I belonged.

That caused a pang. I dumped Butch onto the desk—he screamed again—and headed for the door. The hell with it. I didn't want to hurt. I didn't realize this was going to hurt.

I slammed the door behind me and started walking.

It was a fool thing to do. Reno is high desert country, and survival in August depends on central air-conditioning and heavy consumption of liquids. By the time I walked the few blocks down Mill to Virginia Street, I could have fried eggs on my boot tops, and by the time I reached the air curtain to the Mother Lode, I was flirting with serious dehydration. So I compounded it by doing another fool thing. Instead of going to the coffee shop, I stopped at the first bar and ordered a beer. It felt so good in my throat, cool and bubbly, that I finished it in one long swallow and ordered a second. I sat down, got comfortable, and flagged down the Keno runner. Getting drunk on beer takes a while, but I wasn't in any hurry. I had no place else to be.

An indeterminate time later, a voice said, "You ready to eat yet?"

Standing behind me was a heavyset black man with a gray Afro, red-rimmed eyes, and jowls that gave a new dimension to the word. I wondered how long he'd been there.

"I don't think so, Deke," I told him.

"Well, I am ready to eat, and I saw you just sitting there with that stack of losing Keno tickets, and I thought it sure would be nice to have some company. Need help getting off the stool?"

"I can do it myself."

"I was certain you could, just thought I'd offer."

I stood up a little too quickly to prove my point. I had to grab the bar to keep my body from moving faster than my head could follow. I patted my jeans, trying to remember where I left my wallet.

Deke had it in his hand.

"It was on the bar in front of you," he said. "I used it to settle your tab."

"Thanks."

Telling him to go to hell wouldn't have been gracious.

"If you want to stand there for a while, that's fine, I don't have to go to work for a couple of hours yet."

Deke was a security guard on the graveyard shift. It couldn't have been that late. Nevertheless, I focused on the path between the twenty-one tables that led to the escalator.

Riding up set my brain and body at odds again, and I had to pause at the top. Fortunately, it wasn't far from there to the coffee shop, and I knew where the counter was.

Diane raised her eyebrows when she saw me, but didn't say anything. She just reached for the coffeepot and filled a cup.

"You want some, too?" she asked Deke.

"Coffee is what we want this evening," he said, nodding. "And food. A steak for me, and our friend could use the same."

"I don't think I have enough money." I reached for my wallet to check.

"No, no. Although it's against your principles, I'm paying."

I thought about that and had to sit down.

"I'll pay you back," I said. "I have a check from my mother. I'll cash it tomorrow."

"A check from your mother? You accepted a check from your mother?"

"Hell, yes. You don't think I'd agree to find my father for free."

"Ah. Why, no, of course not. I would never think that of you."

"Good." I took a sip of coffee. It was hot, and I realized I was ready to switch from cold beer to hot coffee. I wondered how long I'd been in the air-conditioning.

"I might think it was a little strange that your mother would pay you to find him, though."

"What? It's because of Al—he's running for the legislature, and Mom doesn't want anybody to know that their marriage isn't quite legal. Danny never signed the divorce papers. She lied to Al and said he did."

Deke chuckled. "Interesting woman, your mother."

"I suppose." I would have to think about that. I didn't see her that way.

I couldn't think very long, because Diane showed up with our steaks, and that distracted me.

"So it be the prospect of looking for your daddy that has you running for cover," Deke said as he picked up his fork.

"He left me."

"Yes, he did. And maybe it be about time you went looking for him to find out why. You could ask him why he left. He might even tell you."

I had to think about that, too.

I was still thinking about it when I got home and passed out on the bathroom floor, right after feeding the cats.

I was still thinking about it when I woke up in bed the next morning, not remembering when I'd left the bathroom. At least, I was thinking about it in the one synapse of my brain that wasn't firing pain signals.

There was aspirin in the bathroom, I knew that. I would take two aspirin, come back to bed, and I would never drink again.

The second time I woke up wasn't as bad. And I wasn't wondering what to do any longer. Deke was right. I had to find Danny and ask him why he left, why he never tried to get in touch with me.

My head was almost clear by the time I got out of the shower. In the closet of the room I use for a living room—the real living room is my office—I had stowed a cardboard box of things that Mom had given me when she and Al had moved to the lake, things I had left in my room when I moved out, that I didn't want to trash, but I didn't want to carry. I was pretty sure I had an old picture of Danny in there.

The box was in a corner, behind a filing cabinet that I ought to clean out one of these days. Even the IRS doesn't make you hold on to more than a few years' worth of records. I still had essays that I wrote for high school English classes.

I lifted the box over the filing cabinet, let it drop gently onto the floor, and sat cross-legged in my bathrobe beside it.

Odd, the stuff that gets kept. A small stuffed penguin— Danny had won that at the Washoe County Fair one year, in the shooting gallery. Those mounted rifles buck so bad it was a wonder he could hit anything. I know—I've tried since, never won. A carved wooden monkey with a broken arm. I had absolutely no memory of that monkey. A cap pistol in a small holster. I remembered that, and how much I wanted a real gun. A photograph of a sullen, flat-chested twelve-year-old, with blond hair hanging in her face, sitting on a beach towel. Had to have been taken at Lake Tahoe, when I was at summer camp. I stopped looking at anything else when I found the photograph of Danny.

I had expected to find that he wasn't as handsome as I remembered. I was ready for that. I wasn't ready to discover that he was every bit as handsome as I remembered.

The picture was the three of us, Danny, Mom, and me. It had been taken at an employee picnic, when Mom was working for the telephone company. Danny had his arm around me—I was maybe fourteen, but my head was already up to his shoulder—and we were both laughing. Mom had kind of a tight smile, as if Danny had done something that embarrassed her, but she was putting up a good front.

I put the photo on the coffee table and returned the rest of the box to its corner behind the filing cabinet. I sat down on the old dark green sofa and stared at the photo some more. The laughing man was a stranger now.

Mom looked almost the same. Her jawline had been a little firmer, and her hair a little darker, but that was the same woman who had been in my office the day before. I had changed, of course—I had lost what little bit of roundness of cheek or shoulder I showed in the picture. If anything, now, I looked more like him. The blond hair, the darker eyebrows, the freckles, the strong bones.

What had Danny been doing that summer? Bartender or auto mechanic? He was good at both, could always find a job, but not so good at staying in one for too long. If he had kept on working as a bartender, maybe the Vegas union would have a record of him. Had to check.

And anyway, it was time to get dressed.

I belong to a computer network of independent PIs who have agreed to run minor errands for each other for free and work out either reduced rates or barter if a big favor is required. Where possible, of course, the other PI's fee is charged full fare to the client. I booted up the computer and sent an E-mail message to Rudy Stapp, a Vegas PI I had worked with before. I was betting he would pick up on last-name's-the-same and wouldn't ask but wouldn't charge me.

I was right on both counts. He didn't get back to me until the next day, and the message on my computer said only that the Vegas local of the bartenders' union had no record of a Danny O'Neal in the active file, but that the secretary was an ex-girlfriend (how many ex-girlfriends did Rudy have? half the secretaries in Las Vegas?) who had agreed to take a look at the dead file.

I also checked with a friend at the DMV. Besides the three in Las Vegas (the initial D. must have stood for something else), she came up with a Daniel in Carson City and one in Winnemucca. No Sam Courter.

I tried the Carson City and Winnemucca numbers. The voice on the Carson City answering machine was thirty years too young, and when I asked the Winnemucca woman in my best professional voice if this was the home of the Danny O'Neal who had been living in Reno in the seventies, and she said no, they had lived in Winnemucca all their lives, I believed her.

Okay. Next stop, the camel races.

Except the camel races were still a week and a half away. At first, I thought about what it would be like when I found Danny. I thought how glad he'd be to see me, imagined him telling me that he had wanted to get in touch, but didn't know how, after all the years. I imagined him embarrassed. I imagined me embarrassed. I imagined me calling Mom and telling her I changed my mind, I was sending back the check. But the gut truth was, I could live with anything but my own cowardice.

I spent a full ten days shooting down Klingons on the computer. Toward the end, I even did it in my sleep.

The celebration of the camel races lasts three days, and if Sam Courter were racing, he'd probably arrive on Friday. But the Friday of the race weekend came and went, and I was still too busy zapping Klingons to get in the Jeep. Same with Saturday. I had to make a move on Sunday. But by then, my mind was settled comfortably in space. The old pain that had suddenly materialized to haunt me was back in suspended animation as I headed south on Highway 395 toward the turnoff that would take me to Virginia City.

Virginia City was built on Wealth. That's easy to forget, when you see the way it looks now. A ghost town, kept alive by tourism, where the only obvious ways to make a living are jeweler, confectioner, souvenir seller, twenty-one dealer, or bartender. But what's there is real, not theme-park fake. Even the coffee shops have crystal chandeliers and flowered oxblood wallpaper, and there are tours of a few of the old mansions available, as well as some working mines. Still, there's a weird mix of The Way It Was Museum on one side of C Street and the tribute to John Wayne on the other, as if reality wasn't enough at some point, or maybe when it comes to John Wayne (and Clint Eastwood and Marilyn Monroe, both displayed prominently in poster shops), the line between myth and reality gets a little blurred. And a plaque marking the spot where "Mark Twain Was Robbed Here" is a bit precious.

Speaking of myth, I have a problem with all the soft porn Julia Bulette stuff. Julia Bulette has become a sort of Happy Hooker legend, the original pro with the heart of gold, when in reality she was murdered for her money at thirty-five. A short and sordid life in a city where not even the statue of

Justice is blind. Prostitution is still legal in Nevada, though, more than a hundred years after Julia Bulette bled to death on her bed, and hanging on racks right next to the Official Camel Race T-shirts commenting "Spit Happens" were ones promising "The Customer Comes First at Mustang Ranch." Sometimes I wonder why I haven't moved out of the state.

Other times I look out at the mountains, and I know why. When I was in second grade or so, I wasn't much good at art, except that I liked to draw mountains. I would have an inch or so of trail at the bottom of the picture, with a few gray and yellow lines beside it meant to be sagebrush, and I'd leave an edge of pale sky at the top, but the rest would be mountains, mountains piled on top of one another, gold to brown to blue to purple, fading back to infinity. There are a couple of bars in Virginia City where you can stand out on the deck and see mountains just like that.

But I wasn't there to look out at the mountains. Except turning away didn't help, because whether looking down the hill toward St. Mary's of the Mountains church or up toward Piper's Opera House, I was distracted by the ghosts of the town. At Piper's Opera House miners watched Shakespeare. A hundred years later we watch MTV. Progress. Although— myth and reality again—the late-show movie memory of Mitzi Gaynor as Lotta Crabtree singing "Dixie" to Dale Robertson with the tears running down her face is what I think of when I see the raked stage and the gilt boxes. I watch a lot of television after midnight, which is why I know Mitzi Gaynor and Dale Robertson.

I knew it was time to face my own ghosts, if only because I couldn't figure out any other choice. I'd had a lot of practice as a teenager, staying in my head when my heart was too sore to be touched. I had a nasty hunch I was going to be doing that again.

I hadn't thought I'd have much trouble spotting one

middle-aged biker, but every man there for the races seemed to be wearing either a Disneyland T-shirt and shorts or a Harley T-shirt and 501s. I hoped Sam Courter would be riding.

I bought a button with a caricature of a camel curling its disdainful lip that was my admission ticket to the race site and walked down the short, dusty street to the roped-off arena.

A beer company was one of the major sponsors of the races, and even at eleven in the morning, both the Disneyland types and the Harley types were lined up at the wagons. I didn't know how long I'd be out there, and still mindful of my last beer on a hot afternoon, decided to stick to soft drinks. They're actually better at preventing dehydration anyway—alcohol, even beer, makes it worse.

The flimsy metal stands facing the dusty, temporary track were starting to fill when I got there. I climbed to the top row, which was empty, because I didn't want to be hemmed in. I discovered that nobody was sitting up there because the bench wasn't level. That was fine—I hadn't expected to be comfortable. I braced myself against one of the periodic poles that sported bright, flapping, triangular pennants.

"Good afternoon, and welcome—" a voice boomed before the sound system went dead. A moment later it was back. "And welcome to the International Camel Races. The races will start at twelve noon, on the dot. So when the races start, check your watches, and set them to twelve noon."

A little Nevada humor there.

The voice introduced a banjo player, who appeared on the grandstand at one end of the arena, dressed like a nineteenth-century tinhorn gambler, and started accompanying himself as he sang old miners' ballads. Actually, he was pretty good. If I hadn't been sitting on a tilted grandstand on a hot afternoon, I would have liked listening to him.

The first four camels were maneuvered into their chutes about quarter after twelve. One of the scheduled riders couldn't be found, and the sponsor had to find a substitute. I listened carefully for the names of the riders, but none of them sounded like real people—except for a Reno disc jockey, whose name had never sounded real. The sponsors were a saloon, a construction company, a whorehouse, and a dentist (the disc jockey was riding for the dentist). They didn't sound real, either. I guess it was just something about the afternoon.

At the sound of a taped bugle, the gates to the chutes were dragged open, and the camels came more or less flying out, jerking their heads against the reins with a lack of enthusiasm that bordered on recalcitrance. The camel jockey from the construction company had reached the finish line before the other three had turned the corner.

A few words from the winner and back to the banjo player. This could be interminable. The damn program didn't even say how many races there were, just that the championship race was at four. I couldn't sit that long.

But I didn't have to. About two-thirty, after I had lost count of how many unhappy camels I had watched refuse to play the game, my attention had wandered to three seven-year-old girls on a nearby slope who obviously thought the banjo music was the real entertainment for the day and danced between races with the freedom that only seven-year-olds seeking attention have. I jerked back to the races when I heard some words on the loudspeaker that came out something like "Sam, Sam the Alamo Man, riding for Betsy Beaufort and her Girls, in chute number two."

Chute number two. The bugle sounded, the gates opened, and the camel from chute number two headed for the wrong corner, saddle slipping slowly, jockey slipping faster. I only caught a glimpse of him before two guys picked him up and helped him limp out of the arena.

He had long gray hair. And he was wearing a sleeveless vest with a Harley insignia on the back.

Chapter
2

MY HOPE OF sitting alone on the top tier and slipping easily away had been foiled by three teenage boys, who grudgingly stood to let me pass. I stomped one's toes by accident. I'm not sure he believed my apology.

Because of the slope, the top row wasn't all that much higher off the ground than the bottom row, so I grabbed the flagpole and swung myself down. I walked behind the VIP/Press box, which only had the advantage of a roof and possibly its own beer keg over the rest of us, and down toward the camel stalls. The muted strain of "Dueling Banjo" (it sounded like hell without the counterpoint) followed me.

I was stopped by a young man in a red T-shirt and jeans at the edge of a roped-off area.

"You're not allowed around the camels without a special pass," he said.

"Oh, hell, Kevin, let me in—I'm looking for Sam Courter."

Kevin Wagner had been at UNR the same time I had. He had come from Yerington, so I hadn't known him before college, and since all we had was one sophomore English class and History of Western Civ together, we weren't really friends. He had gone to work for a Reno bank, in the trust department. UNR students used to joke that Yerington kids were all brain-damaged because of the arsenic in the water supply. I thought of that every time I read about a failing bank.

"Oh, hi, Freddie, I didn't recognize you."

Brain-damaged.

"I can't let you in if you don't have the right pass," he continued, "but I'll try to find Sam. Stay there, and don't let anyone in."

I should have followed him. The task was too complicated to trust him with it.

But he carried it off. It took him about five minutes, but when he came back, he was accompanied by the same limping man with long gray hair and a Harley vest who had fallen off the camel. A folded red bandanna covered his forehead, down to gray eyebrows over dark, narrow eyes. A gray mustache started below a broken nose, curved around his mouth, and drooped to his chin.

"I'm Sam Courter," he said, holding out his hand. "Who's looking for me?"

The hand was hard, attached to an arm with biceps that stood out like boulders. The wings of a tattooed eagle rippled across one as we shook. Sweat ran down his gray-haired chest and along the tanned slope of his beer belly, exposed by the open vest.

"Freddie O'Neal," I answered. "I'd like to talk with you. Can I buy you a beer?"

He nodded. "Let's go."

I walked back the way I had come, Sam limping next to me. He was about three inches shorter, with both of us in boots, but he didn't seem to notice.

The announcer was calling the next race, including a woman jockey, the second of the afternoon, one Brandy

Alexander. I guess we'd made a few strides since Julia Bulette.

"How many years you been doing this?" I asked.

"Except for a couple of years when I was out of the country, I been riding since 1959, the first year they had these races. I wasn't much more than a kid. I lost to John Huston."

That was in the program, about John Huston. The races started because somebody who worked for the Territorial Enterprise, in the spirit of Mark Twain and Dan De Quille, had written up a story about a camel race that didn't happen. Camels had been used to carry ore in the nineteenth century, but there hadn't been camels in Virginia City in decades. Nevertheless, the following year, the *San Francisco Chronicle* offered to sponsor a camel. So, hey—there had to be a real race. John Huston was the *Chronicle*'s jockey, and he won. The races became international when the Australians wanted to join the party.

"So John Huston's dead and you're still racing," I said.

Sam looked at me and didn't say anything.

We got to the wagon and waited for the three Disneyland T-shirts ahead of us to get their beers. I ordered two, paid for them, and handed him one.

"Come on," he said.

I followed him away from the arena, up the dusty slope to the parking lot, and along the second row of cars. He stopped at an aged Winnebago that was taking up two spaces, one for itself and one for a striped awning that gave shade to a couple of faded canvas chairs.

Sam pointed to one and took the other.

"I'm here with friends," he said. "They're still down at the races."

I sat. The chairs were positioned so that the view was

panoramic, sweeping up across mountains and sky and over to St. Mary's, which was just about level with us.

Sam swallowed about a quarter of his beer and waited for me to take it all in and come back.

"I hear you know Danny O'Neal," I said.

"Used to. Haven't seen him in a while. You're his kid."

It wasn't a question.

"How do I find him?"

He shook his head. "If I knew, I'd tell you."

"Then tell me what you do know."

"I know he was on the run from something, and my guess is you won't find him because he doesn't want to be found."

The waxed paper beer cup was already beginning to soften in the heat. And the beer wasn't really cold, and I didn't want it much.

"Start earlier—start from when you first knew him."

"That was Nam, and I don't much want to start there. We met in a Saigon bar, both from Nevada, and we both got back to the States in one piece, give or take some frayed edges. That was just over twenty years ago. That good enough?"

"Yeah, okay."

"Danny went back to Reno, I ended up back in Las Vegas. We agreed to meet at the camel races. He showed for the next few years, even rode one year. Didn't see him often between races, but one afternoon I found him sitting on my doorstep. Said he was thinking about traveling through Mexico for a while, did I want to go. I had some other things going in my life, but I told him to keep in touch. He stopped by twice after that, once on his way back from Mexico— that didn't take long, Danny couldn't talk the language and didn't like Mexicans—and then again a couple of years ago. He was drunk, with a hooker, said he was tired of running and thought he might stay in Vegas. That was the last time I saw him."

Sam finished his beer, crumpled the cup, and hooked it into a trash can next to the open door of the Winnebago. While he was talking, I had been watching a fly die a boozy death in what was left of mine. I placed my cup in the dust next to the chair. He reached down, emptied the beer and the dead fly into the dirt, and lobbed the cup into the can.

"I was going to do that," I said. "I wouldn't have left it."

"Well, I did it for you. You're welcome."

He watched me bristle. This was some kind of a goddamn game, and I wasn't going to play.

"You didn't hear from him in between? That was a lot of years," I said.

"Ten, twelve, I don't know." He was still watching me.

"And you don't know where he is now."

"Not a clue."

"You said he wanted to stop running. From what?"

"Not a clue about that, either."

"Was he running when he went to Mexico? Or when he came back? When did he start?"

Sam shook his head. He looked as if he thought about not answering that one at all, but finally he did. "Danny was always running from his own demons. I don't know when—or if—it got to be more than that."

"What about the hooker? What can you tell me about her?"

"Nothing—but Moira talked to her, might remember her name."

"Who's Moira?"

"A friend. She's down at the camel races now, but she'll probably be back before too long."

"Well, then, you can tell me more about Danny while we're waiting."

He shook his head again and sighed.

"Let up a little, kid. Have you thought about whether you really want to do this? The Danny you find—if you do find him—isn't going to be the Danny you remember."

"How do you know what I remember?"

"I don't, but I could give it a shot. You remember a laughing blond giant of a man who gave you rides on his shoulders when you were a baby and took you to baseball games when you were in junior high, a father who taught you to shoot and swim and throw a ball like a boy, not like a girl. Probably the only bad things you have to say about him are that he made your mother cry a lot, and sometimes you didn't blame him for that, and he left you."

I didn't say anything. Danny didn't teach me to swim, but it was close enough.

"Maybe you remember how much he drank, maybe you don't," Sam continued, "but let me tell you that he did. A lot."

"I don't remember him drunk."

"My guess is you don't remember him sober, not after he got back from Nam. The war didn't change him—just made him more of what he was. He didn't want to fight, drunk or sober, it just didn't hurt as much drunk."

"I thought you didn't want to talk about the war."

"I don't. But you need to know, the last time I saw Danny he was bloated and red-faced, and if he hadn't burned a hole clear through his liver, it wasn't for lack of trying. Kidneys probably weren't worth much, either, so if he's still alive, he isn't pretty."

"Okay. You warned me. I'm still looking for him."

Sam nodded. "Good luck."

He got up and went into the Winnebago, coming back with two bottles of beer. I didn't really want one, but I took it when he held it out because I wanted to say thank you, and that was the easy way.

"You're welcome," he said, nodding again.

We sat in silence, watching in the distance as a camel jockey draped in billowing turquoise polyester, like a cartoon Arab, won his heat.

"How's Ramona?" he asked, still focused on the far arena.

"What? Mom? She's fine. She said she saw you here a few years ago."

He nodded. "She always was a good-looking woman. Hadn't changed much, the years were kind to her. And the guy she was with looked as if he could afford to take care of her."

"That was Al. She married him about a year after Danny split." Something had been bothering me, sitting there. A memory that wouldn't quite surface. "Sam—did I ever meet you before? You're starting to look familiar."

"I came down to your house a few times, slept on the couch. You were usually in bed when I got there. Once you were up getting ready for school when I was still having coffee. You were probably about twelve at the time. I'd be surprised if you remembered."

"I don't, really." I just almost remembered. We settled into silence again, watching the races. "It must be getting on toward the end," I said, after I got tired of trying to remember in the silence. "Don't you want to go down there for the championship?"

"No. I don't much care who wins anymore, as long as it isn't the Aussie bastards. A good thing you caught me this year. I don't know if I'll come back."

"You could come back, just not ride," I said, thinking of how he limped away from the arena.

"Hell, no. I only come for the ride. And because Betsy gives me my choice of her girls, that's still fun."

"How can you say that?" I exploded. "It's goddamn exploitation."

"They don't seem to mind."

"Did you ever ask?"

"Yeah, sure. Right in the middle, I stop and ask. If I have two, I ask them both."

I glowered. "What does Moira say?"

"What?"

"You're up here with Moira—doesn't she care?"

"I'm up here with Moira and Doc, who are my friends. Besides, there ain't no real Betsy, that's a joke. I just wondered how you'd react. You gonna be that hotheaded and judgmental with your daddy—if you find him?"

I had to think about that. How would I react if I found my father drunk, ugly, and in bed with a prostitute half his age? I didn't know. I didn't know how I'd react finding him in any situation, and I still wasn't sure I wanted to find out.

Sam shifted in his chair. Two people were walking toward us through the shimmering afternoon dust, a slender, fortyish woman with long dark hair wearing Levi's, high boots, and a pink Harley T-shirt, alongside a barrel-shaped man a little older, with black-rimmed glasses and a neatly trimmed gray beard, also wearing the inescapable Levi's, a black T-shirt, a vest like Sam's complete with ride buttons, and a motorman's cap over his gray hair.

"Moira, Doc, this is Freddie. She's Danny O'Neal's kid."

I shook the offered hands, Moira's small, leathery one, Doc's beefy one, as Sam set up two more canvas chairs that had been leaning against the side of the Winnebago. He handed Moira his beer—she drained what was left in one gulp—and went inside for more.

"I haven't seen Danny for a couple of years," Moira said.

"I'd ask how he is, but I'd guess you haven't seen him in a lot longer than that."

"Why? Why would you guess that?"

"Because the last time he stopped by, he was talking about settling down, but not about looking up his wife and kid. Did he?"

It came out a little tough, but not unkind.

"No. You're right. He didn't. So I'm looking for him. Can you help me?"

She shook her head. "I don't know how. He was Sam's friend, I only met him once or twice here at the races before he left for Mexico."

I felt a twinge of jealousy, that Moira had been at the races and I hadn't. And I knew it was over Danny, a twinge that this stranger knew him, maybe better than I did.

"Sam said that Danny was with a hooker the last time he stopped by. He said you talked with her, that you might remember her name."

"She wasn't exactly a hooker."

"She was a hooker," Sam growled, handing Moira a fresh beer.

Moira smiled at him, a kind of intimate smile. "Not exactly. She was a dancer. She turned tricks to pay for her dancing lessons, that's all."

"She was a hooker," Sam growled again.

"Some people see things as black or white," Moira said, turning to me. "Sam is one of them."

"She sure as hell wasn't with Danny for his looks or his wit," Sam said.

"If it was for his money, where did he get it?" I asked.

"Good question." Sam raised his eyebrows until they touched the red bandanna. "I didn't ask him."

"Her name," I said to Moira. "Do you remember her name?"

"Jackie. Jackie something."

"That helps," Doc said. I jumped. I hadn't even realized he was listening. "Half the hookers in Vegas are named Jackie something. Or Kathy something, or Jennifer something, or Tiffany something."

"You forgot Tammy something and Bambi something," Sam added.

They snickered together over their beers.

"Sounds like a fucking sorority," I said.

Doc choked and beer exploded out of Sam's nose. He pulled the bandanna off his forehead, wiped the rest of his face with it, and tucked it in his belt. I didn't think the line was that funny.

"You'll be all right." Sam dropped a heavy hand onto my shoulder. "Yeah, you'll be all right."

"I'll think of it at two o'clock in the morning, that's always what happens," Moira said. "Stay for dinner, and we can talk about something else, and maybe it'll creep up on me."

"Thanks, but I ought to get back to Reno."

"Why?"

There really wasn't any reason why I had to leave. But I am not too comfortable around strangers under the best of circumstances, and there was something weird about what was going on here, and it didn't make me feel any better that these were Danny's friends. I had expected a polite refusal to be okay, however, so I didn't know how to answer Moira's question.

"Well—I just hadn't planned on staying," I said lamely, trying not to look away from Moira's eyes, "and it doesn't seem right to bust in on you."

"Don't be silly. We were just going to barbecue a couple of chickens—one isn't enough for the three of us—and there's plenty of potato salad and beer. Please stay."

I didn't see any way out of it.

We drank a couple more beers, and somebody won the camel race championship—we figured the Americans, from the cheers—and the sky got translucent, and the mountains faded from brown to purple, and Moira decided it was time to start the charcoal. Sam and Doc worked together with the ease of friends who had been setting up two portable barbecues, one for each chicken, for years.

"What do you do when you're not watching camel races?" I asked Moira.

"We ride. When we're not riding, we teach. I teach part-time in the UNLV business school. Doc's a tenured full professor in the English department."

"That is a mind-boggler."

"Not really. I teach communications. If you need a job fast, and if you have a degree or two in the humanities, and if you're smart, you figure out how it applies in business. Psychologists teach organizational behavior or marketing, anthropologists teach corporate culture, philosophers teach management or social issues, and English majors teach communications."

"Nobody minds how you live?"

Moira was amused. "Not yet. Although Doc probably wouldn't have gotten tenure if anybody had really been paying attention."

"And you?"

She shook her head. "I'm not up for it. Never finished my Ph.D. And I'll probably have to find something else to do, with all the budget cuts. People like me are the first to go."

"What about Sam?"

"He mostly works in construction, whatever is available, although like me, Sam never got his union card. He started to get a degree in architecture once, and he's learned enough practical stuff over the years that he's a pretty valuable handyman."

"Do you remember the hooker's last name?"

"Trying to catch me off guard? No, I don't remember, and quit bringing it up or I never will. What do you do?"

"I'm a private investigator."

"Really?"

"Really."

"What a hoot! And you're looking for your own father?"

"Yeah. Mom hired me to find him."

Moira thought that was hilarious.

"I guess it does sound pretty ridiculous," I added. There was something about the softening evening and the smoky scent of the charcoal that made it almost inconsequential.

Almost didn't quite make it, though. Her laughter still stung.

"I'm sorry," she said, making an effort to stop. "It's serious, I know, it really is. And it must be painful, too, to dredge up all the memories of him leaving, which you must be doing if you're looking for him."

"Fuck you."

"Okay. I'm really sorry. And I'll think of the hooker's last name, I promise."

I was starting to hurt, and I wished I'd left.

"Freddie? Are you okay?" she added. She was looking at me now, a little more sober.

"Yeah, sure."

"I said I was sorry. I didn't mean to be careless with your life, truly I didn't."

I was about to say "yeah, sure" again, for lack of anything better, but the chickens went onto the barbecue just then, and the flare, smell, and sizzle combined to distract us both. And then I thought to say, "Moira? How well did you really know Danny?"

Moira looked tired. But she shifted suddenly, brightly smiling at me.

"Ellis! That was her name, Jackie Ellis! Do you think finding her will help?"

"Maybe. Thanks."

Sam came over to us and said something, and they talked, and we ate chicken, and finally I got to go home. I traded addresses and phone numbers with them before I left. There was only one for the three of them.

I hadn't put the top on the Jeep for the winter yet, and the drive down the hill and across Washoe Valley to Reno was cool, slow, and sobering.

How the hell was I going to find a Las Vegas hooker named Jackie Ellis? Even if Moira had told the truth?

Chapter 3

THE ANNOYING THING about September mornings in Reno is how balmy they can be, promising a day of gentle sunshine on green-to-gold leaves, with just enough left of the night coolness that I think maybe getting up wouldn't be too bad. Sometimes I'm even in the shower before I remember what a lousy day it is.

The Monday after the camel races I didn't quite make it to the shower. There was a puddle on my kitchen floor that appeared to have developed from the closet shielding my hot water heater. I opened the door and stood, groggily watching the leak and contemplating the joys of owning a house. I pulled on the same jeans and shirt I had worn the day before, attached the garden hose to drain the rest of the water into the backyard, threw a couple of dirty towels into the puddle, and drove down Virginia Street to a discount plumbing-fixtures store. I was too early.

Two cups of bad coffee and a fast food breakfast later, the store opened. I suffered the condescending clerk, the credit-card-busting bill, and the fact that I needed help hoisting the new heater into the Jeep. I was momentarily cheered because the top was still off so the new heater fit, the sun was shining so neither I nor my new hot water heater got

31

rained on, and also because I had a dolly at home so that I didn't need help getting the heater into the house.

Plumbing isn't one of my natural talents, but I had taken a couple of community college how-to courses when I got the house, and installing a hot water tank happened to be one of the things covered. I was in the shower—lukewarm though it was—before noon.

And just as I began to feel better, I remembered what a really bad day it was.

The only lead I had on the whereabouts of Danny O'Neal, my father, was that he was last seen about two years ago, drunk, with a Las Vegas prostitute whose name may or may not have been Jackie Ellis.

I left a telephone message for my friend at the DMV, a computer message for Rudy Stapp, and called Mom. Al answered the phone, which didn't help the day any.

"Ramona's grocery shopping," he said. "I'll have her call you."

We got off the phone as quickly as we could without quite being rude to one another. Mom called back about half an hour later.

"You have to come up with something more," I told her. "There has to be something that you don't realize would help, but it really would make a difference in whether I find him."

"Like what?"

"Well, like a Social Security number or something. Don't you have any old tax returns or anything?"

"Of course not. I destroyed everything I had that reminded me of Danny."

I was sure she had, but that would have been the easy way. I was going to have to do it the hard way.

"All right, I just gave it a shot. Then I need to know what happened right before he left."

"Nothing." She snapped it out the way only Mom can snap a word, as if it were the tip of a bullwhip.

"Come on, Mom. Were you fighting? Was there another woman?" I hated asking her this stuff.

"We were always fighting and there was always another woman. That was why we were always fighting. But as far as I know, he left alone."

"What about money?"

"We fought about that, too. He made it, but never as quickly as he spent it. And I don't remember that he had any more than whatever was left from his current paycheck when he disappeared."

"Can you think of anything Danny might have been running away from? Was there anything that happened before he left—maybe even something that didn't have anything to do with us—that would have scared him into running?"

"If it didn't have anything to do with us, how would I know about it?"

"Didn't the two of you talk?"

"Not much." Snap, snap, went the bullwhip.

"Okay. Then what about friends besides Sam Courter? Friends here in Reno? Didn't he hang out with anybody?" I was starting to feel desperate.

"Did you find Sam? What happened?"

"I found him. He hasn't seen Danny in years. He asked about you."

"Did he? That was nice of him. Well, I can't think of any other friends. Can you? You probably went places with him as much as I did."

I had thought about that before I called her. It seemed to me that Danny knew everybody, wherever we went, but he didn't have any friends.

"What about where he worked?" I asked, hedging her question. "What were the last couple of places?"

"There was an automotive shop on Glendale Boulevard that's closed now—I don't remember the name—and before that he was a bartender at the Old Corral, a cowboy bar on Highway 395, about halfway to the community college."

"Yeah, I know where it is."

"But I can't imagine anyone who knew Danny is still there."

"You're probably right."

None of this was making me feel any better.

"Are there any relatives he might have contacted?"

"Who? His father died when he was thirteen, his mother died the year we got married, and he was an only child. If he had any cousins, he never mentioned them."

I knew that, but I was somehow hoping she would disclose the existence of a long-lost uncle or something. We had been the nuclear family reductio ad absurdum, with a void on my father's side and strained relationships on my mother's. I had always envied kids with grandparents and siblings and cousins, big family Christmases and somewhere embracing to go when it got rough at home.

"I'm sorry I haven't been more help," Mom continued when I didn't say anything. "But you're so resourceful, Freddie, I know you can find him without me." She was cooing at me, something I have always found annoying. "Why don't you think what you would do, if you wanted to drop out of sight? That's probably better than anything I could come up with."

I wanted to explain to her that, as far as I knew, disappearance was not a genetic trait. But hell, it might be. At the moment it didn't sound so bad.

We agreed to call if either of us thought of anything.

I got off the phone with her midafternoon, and I felt worse than I had when I got up.

I waited until dark before I left for the Old Corral. Monday would be a quiet night—they had live entertainment on the weekends, when the cowboys, both real and urban, were hanging out, but I half expected to be the only person there on a Monday. I was the only person on Highway 395 North once I left the city limits, although a couple of cars passed me going south, toward town. Probably teachers leaving the community college late.

The community college occupied the buildings where the Air Force base used to be—one of those rare cases when government planning really worked. I would have expected the federal boys to let the old buildings rot while the state boys raised taxes to build their own new ones. But sometimes they surprise you.

The Old Corral had survived all changes. The neon sign had been there as long as I remembered, and if they ever took it down, it should go into a museum of popular culture somewhere. The words were spelled out in loops of golden rope, with a white hat topping the "O," a pair of red and brown boots filling out the "RR," and a green saguaro cactus behind the final "L," which was a little silly, since the bar was six or seven hundred miles north of the nearest natural saguaro. Bright red letters at the bottom said "beer" and "music."

I was almost the only person there. When I parked, three other cars were in the large lot—bigger than the building—actually two cars and a battered yellow pickup truck. And three other people were in the saloon, four if you counted the bartender. A man in his sixties was sitting at the far end of the bar, watching what sounded like football on a small television set perched next to a beer bottle. A man of indeterminate age—all I could see was his hat silhouetted against the orange glow of the jukebox—was jingling some coins, as if he might prefer a tune to the sports announcers' muted calls. And a woman of sad middle age was sitting at a table with two beers, looking at the man in the hat, waiting for him to pick out a song and come back.

The bar was a long one, and the bartender looked as if he should have had company back there. The small tables started a few feet away, arranged in a U around a dance floor and a darkened bandstand with a set of traps in one corner. The whole room was pretty dark, although it was helped some by the mirror behind the bar and by the collection of neon beer signs reflected in it.

I sat down at the bar and ordered a beer in response to the bartender's nod. I usually avoid looking at myself in mirrors, but I was stuck, at least until he brought my beer. I was facing a woman with long, coarse blond hair, caught by a rubber band at the back of her neck, wearing a denim jacket. The light was too dim for me to see my eyes, which are listed on my driver's license as hazel, or my freckles. I could see my square jaw.

The bartender slapped the glass in front of me. He looked about my age, shaggy sandy hair and mustache, big glasses tinted to hide one slightly wandering eye, and a wide leer. Too young to remember Danny O'Neal, but I gave it a shot anyway.

"How long ago was he here?" the bartender asked.

"Mid seventies. I'm not sure of the exact dates."

He shook his head.

"Mid seventies, I was in high school in Tonopah," he said, still leering. "But the place hasn't changed hands since then. Maybe if you talk to the owner, Cliff Farrell, he could help you. Be in on Wednesday. He still works the bar on my night off."

"Thanks."

"Who? Who you looking for?"

The rasp came from the man with the television set.

"Danny O'Neal," I said.

"Danny O'Neal. Big blond Irish drunk. Eye for the ladies."

I stiffened, but managed a polite "That's the guy."

"Sure, I remember him. What the hell ever happened to him? Where'd he go?"

"I'm not sure. I'm looking for him." I was still polite. I picked up my glass and walked down to his end of the bar, smiling. "Can I buy you a beer?"

"Not if you think you're going to get something for it. Why do you want to find Danny O'Neal?"

"He's my father."

"Shit. I'm sorry. Forget what I said. I was thinking about somebody else."

"I don't think so." I held out my hand. "I'm Freddie O'Neal."

"Gary Hanrahan."

The hand that shook mine was firm and callused. I looked into faded blue eyes that had long ago given up any pretensions of a surrounding whiteness. The irises floated in a sea of pink and yellow. His flaring red nose, shining in the light of the small television screen, had suffered slings and arrows to both capillaries and cartilage. Gray hair, slicked away from an old-fashioned part above his left temple, popped into curls above his right temple and around his ears.

"Did you know my father well?"

"I knew him. Here, and at the Bunkhouse, too, when he was bartender there. Right after he came back from the service."

"That was a long time."

He nodded. "But it doesn't mean I knew him well."

"When was the last time you saw him?"

"I'd have to think." He did a terrific job focusing his eyes, looking at me. "Are you coming back on Wednesday? To talk with Cliff?"

"I plan on it."

"Okay. I'll see you then. Seven o'clock."

He switched off his television set, dropped a fiver on the bar, said "See you" to the bartender, and left.

The bartender picked up the bill. "Earliest Gary's left in over a year. What'd you say to scare him?"

"I wish I knew."

I pulled out my wallet, but he raised his hand.

"Gary only had two, so I figure yours is paid for."

"Thanks."

"You're welcome. Come back anytime."

The man in the hat and the sad woman were dancing slowly to mournful, if tinny, sounds of lost love from the jukebox as I left. Outside, the pickup truck was gone from the lot. I drove back to Reno nursing the sting of Hanrahan's memory of Danny. I hoped somewhere somebody would remember him kindly.

When I turned on my computer the next morning, there was a message from Rudy Stapp in response to my inquiry about a hooker named Jackie Ellis: "Are you kidding?" A return phone call from my friend at the DMV was equally fruitless. For all I accomplished in the next two days, I might as well have just paced the floor until it was time to go back to the Old Corral. I thought about going to the Bunkhouse, the bar Gary Hanrahan had mentioned, but Danny hadn't worked there in close to twenty years, and it seemed an even less likely source of information then the Old Corral. Besides, the Bunkhouse was the kind of bar where any woman by herself was available by the hour and had a room upstairs waiting, and I didn't feel like dealing with the kind of flak I'd get in there unless I had to.

I drove back to the Old Corral early Wednesday evening. There were more cars in the lot this time, but no yellow pickup. I hoped Gary Hanrahan was driving something else. Or maybe he was just late.

In either case, he wasn't at the bar. Maybe a dozen guys were scattered along it, in groups of twos and threes, and there were maybe a half-dozen couples sitting at tables. Two more were on the dance floor, swaying to another wail of mournful love from the jukebox. I knew it was different because the last one had been a man, and this was a woman.

I have tried to like country music, mostly because the only time I was ever really in love, the guy liked country music, but it all sounds the same to me. I am one of those who thought there was more truth than humor in the joke that was going around a while ago, about what you hear when you play country music backward: The guy gets his dog, his truck, and his woman.

The man behind the bar was a bigger, bulkier version of Gary Hanrahan who had given up trying to slick down his curly gray hair. And his eyes were pink, yellow, and brown.

I waited until he brought my beer before I asked, "Gary Hanrahan not in yet?"

"Haven't seen him tonight."

"You're Cliff Farrell? You own the place?"

He nodded and waited.

"I'm looking for a man who used to be a bartender here, maybe fifteen years ago. Danny O'Neal. Would you remember him?"

"Sure, I remember him. You his kid?"

"Yeah." I hadn't figured out whether looking so much like Danny—or like Danny used to look—was going to help or hinder. Certainly, it was something I couldn't deny.

"I dunno. I dunno if I remember anything that would help you, and I dunno if I would tell you anyway. You probably don't want my advice, but I think you're better off letting him go. He's been gone a long time. Do something else with your life."

"I'll think about that. At the same time, I'd appreciate it if you'd call and let me know if you can remember anything about Danny." I handed him my card.

"A private investigator? No shit?"

"No shit."

He put the card in the pocket of a rust-colored flannel shirt.

"If I remember anything I think you ought to know, I'll call."

He moved down the bar, back at work. I nursed the beer I had, ordered one more, and Gary Hanrahan still didn't show up. One of the cowboys tried to strike up a conversation, and Farrell shooed him away. I could have done it myself, but it was still a nice thing for him to do. Otherwise, I listened to the jukebox. In fact, I put a dollar in and picked out three Johnny Cash oldies. I can relate to Johnny Cash. Being a Boy Named Sue can't be too different from being a Woman Named Freddie. And he found his father.

At the end of my second beer, I motioned Cliff Farrell over and asked if he knew how I could get in touch with Gary Hanrahan. He had absolutely no idea and suggested that I try the bar again in the next night or two. When I left, there was still no yellow pickup in the parking lot.

If I hadn't been brooding, I would have been driving too fast to catch the flash of yellow in my headlights as I rounded a curve about a mile and a half away from the bar. Whatever the yellow thing was, it was just off to the left and down a slope. I made an illegal—and dangerous, that close to the curve—U-turn, shifted into four-wheel drive, and bounced off the road.

The battered yellow pickup truck was in a gully, leaning against a boulder that would have hidden it from anyone driving north. I parked the Jeep so that its headlights shone into the cab. Gary Hanrahan was slumped over the steering wheel.

I couldn't tell from looking at him whether he was alive or dead. I had to touch his neck, to feel for a pulse.

He groaned, and blood spurted from his mouth onto my hand.

"Oh, hell." I jumped back, composed myself, and gently patted his shoulder. "Gary, I'm going to have to leave to get help. I'll be back as soon as I can. Try not to move."

He groaned again. More blood.

I sprinted back to the Jeep, wiping the blood off on my jeans, from lack of anything else. I had to follow the gully for about a half mile before the slope eased enough for me to make it up to the road. The Old Corral had the nearest telephone. I pulled up in front of the building, left the engine running as I hopped out, pushed the door open, and yelled into the barroom.

"Gary Hanrahan's had an accident. His truck's in a gully, about a mile and a half back toward Reno. Call an ambulance. I'll leave my Jeep on the highway with the lights on."

I barely waited for Farrell to nod before I let the door swing shut and hopped back into the Jeep.

I drove slowly and carefully until I reached the curve and saw the truck. Then I made another quick U and, as promised, left the Jeep on the highway with the headlights on. I had a small flashlight in the glove compartment, but the beam was too fragile and easily swallowed by the dark, downhill landscape. I made a mental note to replace it with something more substantial on my next trip to a hardware store.

Fortunately for my vision, if not for Gary's chances of rescue, we were far enough from the city that the stars and a gibbous moon had no neon haze to contend with. Once my eyes adjusted, the sandy slope appeared almost white, except where the scrub cast black shadows. I stuck the flashlight in the waistband of my jeans and half walked, half slid down to the gully, digging in the heels of my boots to keep my balance.

Gary Hanrahan was still slumped over the wheel. This time I reached in for his hand. I didn't have to check for a pulse in his wrist—his fingers tried to close over mine, but he didn't quite have the strength to finish the gesture.

"Gary, it's Freddie O'Neal." I realized I hadn't told him the first time, and he might want to know who was with him. "Cliff Farrell is calling for an ambulance. We'll get you out of here. Just hang in until the medics arrive."

A rasping breath, a faint sound. I didn't have enough light to see if there was more blood spurting from his mouth.

A car engine stopped on the road above us.

"Yo!" someone called.

"Down here!" I yelled back. I jerked out the flashlight and waved it frantically. The beam hit the bulky figure of Cliff Farrell at the top of the slope.

"Not in my eyes, fergoshsake. I can see better without it."

I flicked it off and watched him traverse the slope in much the same way I had, sliding and digging in his heels.

"How is he?" Farrell asked when he reached the truck. He was breathing hard, so out of shape that the little bit of exertion had gotten to him.

"Bleeding from the mouth. A rib may have punctured his lung. I don't think we should try to move him."

Farrell nodded. "I called the state police, they said they'd get somebody here."

"What about your bar?"

"I called Hardy, told everybody they were on their honor until he got there. Most of 'em know Gary, it'll be okay."

"Hardy?"

"Hardy McCullen, the bartender. I was lucky he was home. But I woulda come anyway. I've known Gary a lot of years."

"You're friends?"

"Probably not that, but he's been drinking at my bar so long that we oughta be."

"Yeah. He said he remembered Danny—gotta be at least fifteen years."

Farrell looked at me as if he had just remembered why I came into the bar.

"Gotta be," he said.

A loud animal wail from Hanrahan startled both of us.

"Hang on, damn it," Farrell ordered, as if Hanrahan might hear him and obey. "The ambulance is coming. Don't die yet, you old bastard."

The wail was followed by a series of jerky moans. I didn't have to see the blood that was coming up with them.

"Hell," Farrell said. "He isn't going to make it."

The moans stopped. Farrell leaned into the cab. When he turned back, his hand was as bloody as mine had been earlier. He wiped the blood onto his shirt, shaking his head.

"Gone."

I sat down on the ground, my back against a boulder. Farrell leaned against the truck, head lowered. We waited in silence.

The fire department ambulance was there almost immediately. Someone turned a searchlight on, bathing us all in a stark whiteness. Farrell's face looked green, and there was a

dark smear on his shirt. Two paramedics with a stretcher
plunged down the slope. One of them opened the door to the
truck and gently eased Hanrahan's body out. They arranged
him on the stretcher, and the one who had touched him first
turned to me.

"You found him?"

I nodded.

"You're going to have to wait for the sheriff, make a
statement. This wasn't just an auto accident. He was shot."

Chapter

4

FUCK DEATH. I hate it. It's not fair, I want to fight it, argue with it, and there's nothing to hit, nothing tangible to connect with, and no one to answer my angry shouts. Shouting at death is as futile as King Canute trying to face down the tide—which was probably just Canute having his little joke, playing with futility, mocking the illusion of royal power. Death is the last joke, the final futility for kings and truck drivers and PIs alike. We travel our short paths, we think we're getting somewhere, feeling almost hopeful, in control, and then bang-bang, somebody's dead.

I wanted to shake Gary Hanrahan, beg him to come back, promise to bring his murderer to justice, if only he would tell me who it was. If only I could turn back the tide. And if only Gary Hanrahan would tell me what he knew about my father.

Farrell had told the paramedics that we would wait for the sheriff at the bar. They didn't have a problem with that. And actually, the state cops—who had come because Farrell had phoned it in as an accident—pulled up just as we were about to leave, and they didn't have a problem with that either. In fact, they thought we had already trampled the scene and interfered with evidence a little too much. I didn't bother reminding them that it hadn't occurred to either Farrell or me that Hanrahan had been shot.

My guilt over having stood there as Hanrahan bled to death had been assuaged only a little by the paramedic's assurance that Hanrahan had been hemorrhaging internally, and there was nothing I could have done. Not moving him was, really, the best policy. The paramedic couldn't do anything about the other piece of guilt. I had a nagging fear that Hanrahan might have been shot to keep him from telling me something. Dumb, sure. Probably coincidence, that Hanrahan had been murdered on his way to meet me.

If it had happened inside the city limits, I could put it down to random violence. In the country during deer season, a hunter's stray bullet. But nobody could mistake a yellow pickup truck for a mountain lion, not even at twilight. Somebody had wanted to kill Gary Hanrahan.

The Old Corral was quiet when Farrell and I walked in, and the few people left stared at us, him with his stained shirt, me with my stained jeans. When somebody asked, "How's Gary?" and Farrell said, "Dead," a couple of "shits" and "hells" accompanied a mass reaching for wallets and settling of bills.

I sat down at a table near the bar. Farrell picked up two drafts and joined me. We still didn't have anything to say to each other. Once the room had cleared, Hardy McCullen poured himself a draft, left the bar, and sat in the third chair. They were old-fashioned wooden chairs, with rounded backs. Something about them was comforting, maybe just that they were old and worn and a lot of people had drunk beer in them over the years.

"Goddamn, that's really too bad about Gary," McCullen said. "What happened? Somebody else involved? He's been driving that road so many years . . ."

McCullen looked from Farrell to me. I waited for Farrell to say it.

"Somebody shot him. Somebody with a rifle was waiting on top of the bluff, shot him as he came around the curve. Bullet hit him in the lung, he bled to death."

"Oh, shit, no." McCullen shook his head, took a deep swallow of beer in the silence. "Who'd do a thing like that?"

"You guys knew him," I said. "Did he have any enemies?"

"Hell," McCullen said. "I don't think he even had any friends. Came in here just about every night, always by himself. On nights when there was a game he wanted to see, he'd bring that little television set. Always drank draft, never talked much to anybody."

"Was he here last night?"

"No, he wasn't. I didn't see him after he left Monday."

"What did he do with his days?"

McCullen shrugged.

"He had an Army pension," Farrell said. "Picked up an occasional handyman job, but he was pretty much retired."

The silence settled around us again like a blanket of cold fog. I was sorry about Hanrahan's murder, and part of me wanted to do something about it, because I had found him. But the larger question for me was whether or not it had anything to do with my search for Danny. If it didn't, I should stay out of the way and let the sheriff handle it. If it did, I was involved whether I wanted to be or not. I hadn't come to any conclusions when two sheriff's deputies walked in.

They introduced themselves as Maddox and Stout. Maddox took the fourth chair at the table, and Stout swung one around from an adjoining table, sitting a little away from the group. They both declined McCullen's offer of a beer.

I told them how I happened to find Hanrahan, why I was supposed to be meeting him, and Farrell added the little he had already said about Hanrahan's life.

"Think the murder has anything to do with your investigation?" Maddox asked. His light coffee skin was only a little darker than his uniform, which didn't camouflage a weight lifter's build. He was maybe thirty years old, and he had kind eyes, unusual for a cop. He'd probably lose the kindness in a few years. Stout was smaller and younger and paler, seemingly along for the ride. Or maybe to learn the trade.

"I wish I knew," I answered.

Maddox nodded. "You do know you have to back away, O'Neal, and let us look into the murder."

My turn to nod.

"If, in the course of pursuing another road to finding your daddy, you should happen to come across some evidence that might relate to Gary Hanrahan's death, we expect you to let us know." Maddox actually smiled at me.

"Yeah, sure. Can I expect reciprocity?"

His smile turned into a chuckle. "Probably not, but we'll see."

They left shortly after. McCullen refilled our glasses. I was going to have to be careful that this case didn't grease the slide into the quicksand of alcoholism.

That's one of the problems of being the child of an Irish drunk—you have to wonder if there's a genetic predisposition toward losing control. And one of the troubles with America is that alcoholism is culturally defined, and we're such a blend of cultures that we've never been able to decide just what it is. We know a drunk when we see one. But is he (or she) an alcoholic? And what would it mean to say that she (or he) is? As far as I'm concerned, drinking (or whatever your painkiller of choice) isn't a problem as long as it doesn't interfere with your work or your relationships. And I didn't have any relationships to worry about. I took a sip of the beer. If it interfered with work, I'd notice.

"I'm going." Farrell chugged his beer. "I'll pay you overtime if you want to stay, or give you another night off. If you want to close and go home, do it."

He tried to push his chair back, but he wasn't steady enough, and it fell as he got up. McCullen and I watched him leave.

"You going to do what the cop asked?"

"No reason not to," I said. Even through the tinted glasses, I could see that one eye of his jump. I looked into his good eye. "For now, I'll figure that what happened to Hanrahan didn't have anything to do with me or with Danny."

"So where do you go next?"

"I don't know. Home to feed my cats, I guess."

"That ain't what I meant and you know it. I just wondered if you had any other leads."

"Not really."

The door to the bar opened, and two couples walked in, the men in jeans and work shirts, the women in spandex and glitter.

"Hey, Hardy," one of the men said. "What're you doing here tonight? Sitting on the wrong side of the bar, and with a pretty girl at that."

"Couldn't stay away," McCullen answered. He turned to me. "I gotta go back to work. I'd close up, but I can use the money. Don't be a stranger. I'd like to hear what happens."

I couldn't figure if he really cared or was just being a good bartender, picking up new customers. And I was too tired to point out to anybody that I was neither pretty nor a girl. So I just thanked him. I listened to McCullen joke with the boys until the jukebox started. I finished my beer and left.

Even though it was still early, once I had gotten out of my bloody jeans and showered and fed the cats, I was too drained to do anything but curl up in my bathrobe and turn the television on. It was some kind of reenactment of some kind of crime, narrated by a Real Cop. I couldn't follow it, though. My mind kept wandering back to an old man bleeding to death in his truck. And that he had left the bar early after talking to me and never made it back again. What if he told someone that Danny O'Neal's kid was looking for him? What if he said he was going to give the kid some information? What if someone didn't want me to have that information? Too many what-ifs. And nothing to attach them to. I'd just have to try the Bunkhouse.

And there was one more thing I could do. I could go down to the morgue—the other morgue, the *Herald*'s morgue—and nose around a little, see what was happening in Reno when Danny disappeared. Probably not very useful, but it would give me the illusion of activity.

I had to get up and stretch, try to bounce out some of the tension. Sundance was sleeping on a sweatshirt at the foot of the bed, so it didn't disturb him, but Butch had been on my lap, and he was so insulted at being moved that he twitched his gray plume of a tail at me and stalked out in the general direction of the kitchen. I reached over and scratched Sundance's exposed stomach, wanting one cat to love me, and he responded by rolling onto his back, encouraging me with a purr, and snagging my sweatshirt with his claws.

Exercising didn't help. I opened a beer and was surprised to discover that it wasn't eleven yet. I picked up the phone.

Sandra answered on the second ring.

"What's wrong?" was her response to my hello.

"Why does something have to be wrong?"

"Because you don't call this late unless something is, even though you know I'm always up until after midnight."

"Nothing, really. I'm going to be hanging out at the *Herald* tomorrow, looking for the spring of 1978, and I thought I'd see if you wanted to have lunch."

"Sure. What happened in 1978?"

"I have no idea. But that's when my father left Reno, and somebody just got killed tonight, and I have to see if anything fits together."

"Goddamn it, why didn't you call me earlier? We've missed the deadline for the morning edition. Who got killed? What happened? I can probably still make the final."

"Shit, Sandra, that's what I love about you. You never lose track of what's really important in life."

Sandra Herrick was the smartest reporter on the *Herald* staff, and her work was her life. I still hadn't figured out how she managed to have a husband and a small child as well. We had sort of known each other since high school, but she had been a cheerleader and one year ahead of me, and I had been ignored by everybody except the National Honor Society, so we hadn't exactly been friends. At UNR I used to see her starring in plays, and we had a couple of classes together, but we still weren't what you would call friends. I wasn't quite certain how we had become friends since. I knew it had started as a matter of professional reciprocity, but I also knew it had become more than that. We liked each other.

"True. That's why you called. What's going on?"

"That's just it. I don't know."

I told her as much as I did know, about Gary Hanrahan, about Mom wanting me to find Danny O'Neal.

"Okay," she said when I was through. "I'll look for you about noon."

I started back to the bedroom, but decided to make one more call.

Mom answered on the second ring, too.

"What's wrong?"

"Nothing, damn it."

"You never call this late unless something's wrong."

I hate being that predictable.

"I just wondered if you remembered the date Danny left town."

"The date? Why would I remember the date?"

"I don't know, Mom. I just thought you might, that's all."

There was a long pause before she answered.

"March 18, 1978. The day after St. Patrick's Day. He had been gone all day, and then all night, and when he came home in the morning we had a fight about how rotten he was. He left and didn't come back."

"Thanks."

Having a plan for the morning made it easier to sleep that night. Although I still had a nightmare about blood on my hands, and every time I wiped it off on my jeans, it appeared again, until I was swimming in blood. I woke up swimming in guilt, that I had been there, standing there while Gary Hanrahan bled to death, and I hadn't done anything to help. If I had known he had been shot, I could have done something. Hell, I probably would have asked him to talk, and he would have died sooner, trying. More guilt.

I left for the *Herald* offices about nine, walking. The morning was bright, a blue-skied eighty degrees, and it was only about a mile to the old building. March 17, 1978. It wouldn't be hard to find out what happened March 17, 1978. I could even go back to the fifteenth or the sixteenth.

The security guard in the lobby directed me down the stairs to public reference. A bubbly young woman with long straight dark hair who looked vaguely familiar asked what I wanted.

"March 17, 1978," I told her.

I introduced myself, and she told me her name. Roseanne Urrutia. One of the many Urrutia sisters. I didn't tell her that I'd had a crush on her brother Kenny—the only boy in the family—in high school. She showed me to the files. Literally, the drawers of microfiche. I found the box I wanted, inserted the spool into the machine, and adjusted the focus.

I reeled from March 17 back to the middle of February, and then forward to early April. Israeli forces moved into Lebanon, we gave away the Panama Canal, the Dow was at 762.56. Joe Frazier was coming out of retirement to fight Kallie Knoetze in Las Vegas, the Equal Rights Amendment was going to be on the primary ballot in June, the weather was clear, and there was the usual assortment of auto accidents and burglaries.

A little before noon I thanked Roseanne for her help and asked the way to the rest rooms. I couldn't even think about eating lunch without washing the dust from my hands. The blood was more of a problem.

When I returned to the lobby, I asked the security guard to buzz Sandra for me. He passed on the message that she would be right down.

Sandra swept into the lobby in a pearl-gray lightweight wool suit, every single ash-blond hair in place, makeup perfect. The guard almost fell over his desk rushing to open the door for us. For her, really. She flashed a perfect smile at him as we left.

By tacit consent, we avoided the subject of importance until we were seated in Harrah's coffee shop and had ordered a couple of salads. One thing about eating with Sandra, I was more likely to order vegetables than at any other time in my life, just to avoid a lecture.

"Okay," she said when the waitress had left. "Did you find what you were looking for?"

"I don't know. I don't know what I was looking for, so I don't know if I found it."

"Let me try again. What did you think might be in the newspapers?"

"Something that would help me figure out why Danny left when he did. Mom insists that nothing unusual was going on, that the fights were the ones they always had. I know she could be lying, but I'd rather believe her. Besides, both Sam and Moira seemed to think he had been running from something, and Gary Hanrahan had something to tell me. I can't imagine he was hesitating over a domestic quarrel that happened more than fifteen years ago."

I picked up a Keno ticket, marked eight numbers, pulled a dollar out of my pocket, and placed it at the edge of the table.

"Why—" Sandra started.

"Don't," I said. Vegetables were one thing—she might be right about them. Giving up Keno was another. A runner grabbed my ticket within seconds. "Anyway, I thought maybe if he had committed some kind of crime, I could spot it, even if he hadn't been suspected of it."

"You mean you thought you could see a fifteen-year-old newspaper story about a bank robbery and say, 'That's the one—my father stuck up that bank at gunpoint and left town.'"

"Not quite that dumb, but almost."

Sandra shook her head. "Statute of limitations. At this point, the only one that hasn't run out is murder."

"I know." I couldn't face that. I pulled out a new Keno ticket, without even knowing what happened with the old one. Usually I play the same one through a meal, even though I always mark the numbers at random. People who mark the same numbers, birthdays or whatever, risk walking into a casino, looking up at the Keno board, and discovering that they just missed winning $50,000.

"I'm sorry, Freddie. That was thoughtless, and I promise I don't think your father was a murderer. Although maybe it was an accident."

I glared at her.

"I'm sorry," she said again.

The waitress brought our salads and Sandra's iced tea. We were quiet until she refilled my coffee cup and left.

"What are you going to do next?" She smiled brightly, but I couldn't help her lighten the mood.

"Keep going backward. Tonight I'll hit the Bunkhouse. And tomorrow I'll call Mom again. What I'm realizing— and this is the truly awful part—is that I don't know anything about my father. He was around for most of my childhood, and I don't think I know who he was."

Sandra gave up trying to cheer me. It was the only lunch I ever had with her that I didn't leave feeling a little better, however grudgingly. But what I had to look forward to— still feeling that Gary Hanrahan's blood was on my hands— was the Bunkhouse that evening, and my mother the next day.

The Bunkhouse took up most of the ground floor of an old, narrow three-story brick building a couple of blocks east of downtown, in an area that had never seen better days. There was a separate door to provide an entry for the two floors above. Rooms available by the month, week, day, or hour. Towels and cockroaches included, but bring your own soap.

Although it was only a mile or so away from my house, close enough that I could have walked, I didn't, in one of my rare prudent decisions. I found a parking place within a half block and stood, looking at the flickering red-orange neon sign, wondering why the hell Danny had been working there. A hand-lettered sign illustrated by a crudely drawn naked woman with huge tits promised Live Entertainment. It was an ugly place, and I didn't want to go in. I pushed open the scarred hardwood door, hoping I wouldn't have to stay long.

The barroom was so dimly lit that it took me a moment to realize how full it was. And quiet, it was quiet for a room with that many people in it. But the sound level changed with a sudden drumroll. The lights went up on one end of the room, a curtain was drawn back jerkily, as if someone was pulling old, frayed ropes by hand, and a short man in a poorly fitting tuxedo stepped to a microphone, the old-fashioned standing kind. Even if his brown toupee had been better, the lines in his face would have given his age away. As would his opening line: "Good evening, ladies and germs."

A heavy presence next to me whispered in my ear, "I need to see your ID."

He wanted my driver's license. What he got was my PI's license. A flashlight lit up first the license, then my face. I couldn't see him, but I could tell from the way he blotted out the surrounding dimness that he was big, and from the halo of the flashlight on his hand that he was black.

"What do you want?" he asked quietly, his voice under-cutting the overmiked emcee.

"Just a private citizen looking around," I answered.

"Ten-dollar cover charge, two-drink minimum, you're on your own if anybody tries to hit on you, and I don't want no violence."

"I hear you. This place mostly regulars?"

"Not a lot of new faces. We get some."

"Anybody been coming here for twenty years?"

"Shit, girl. How would I know?"

Before I could reply, there was another drumroll, the old

joker backed off the stage to scattered applause, a strobe light started flashing, and on slinked a woman in a dark red halter dress with brown hair falling into her face.

"I'm not bad," she whispered, "I'm just drawn this way."

The crowd hooted. It was true, she could have modeled for Roger Rabbit's wife Jessica. But bad or not, she wasn't born with those breasts and that waistline. The cost of creating them probably put a plastic surgeon's child through graduate school. Maybe two.

My jaw must have dropped, because I heard a chuckle next to me.

"Why don't you just tell me what you're doing here? You sure didn't come to watch the show."

"I'm looking for a guy who used to be a bartender here, a long time ago, one Danny O'Neal."

"I never heard of him, and the only person who's been here longer than me is old Ev."

"Who's old Ev?"

"Everett Watson, old pee-stink, the emcee. And if you want to talk to him, I guess you'll have to watch the show after all." He flicked the flashlight on, pointed at the floor. "There's standing room at the bar."

I followed the beam of the flashlight as it guided me toward a narrow space between two bar stools, both weighted down by what smelled like men who had been sweating into their cheap sport coats for several days.

I'd like to be able to say that I didn't watch the show, that I stared at my beer with my back to the stage for the next forty-five minutes or so while four surgically altered women whose only apparent talent was the ability to withstand pain panted a lot and took their clothes off, one at a time. But I got caught by it, the way I once picked up a book of Goya's sketches of war and had to keep turning the pages. I wasn't offended as much as I was saddened by the grotesque flesh.

There had to be tragedies onstage—nobody ever decides when she's a kid that she wants to be a stripper in a seedy bar when she grows up.

The guy on the stool to my left was breathing heavier than the woman on the stage. His hand brushed against my thigh, returned, and attempted to stay. I removed it by twisting his little finger not quite hard enough to pop it out of its socket. The bouncer had said he didn't want violence, and since I couldn't quite decide whether the guy's hand was responsible for a world in which some women made a living by mutilating themselves and then displaying the results to titillate a room full of mouth-breathers, and I wasn't willing to take on the bouncer unless I had to, I let it go.

The emcee closed the show by reminding everyone that the girls would be back at nine-thirty, and a new cover charge would apply to anyone caught staying. The lights went out on the stage area, but came up only slightly in the rest of the room.

I settled my tab, making a mental note to add it to Mom's bill, and looked to my right, hoping the bouncer would be in that direction, so that I wouldn't have to deal with the guy whose finger I had twisted. The bouncer was standing by the door, absorbing light like a hole in space, seeing who stayed and who left between shows.

"How do I get backstage?" I asked.

He didn't even glance at me. "You don't. But don't worry—Ev'll be at the bar by the time you turn around."

"What's his name again?"

"Ev Watson. He drinks Old Crow."

"Thanks."

He was almost right. Watson was through the curtains and a couple of feet short of the bar when I turned around.

Leaning distance—the shot glass was waiting when his hand reached out for it.

The glass was drained and refilled by the time I was close enough to ask if I could talk to him for a moment. He was even shorter offstage. I asked looking down at the bad toupee.

"I don't do the hiring, honey—you'll have to talk to the manager," he answered.

"I already have a job, Mr. Watson." I said it patiently. I've learned to be patient when I want something from a man who doesn't understand that he just insulted me. But sometimes it's tough. Particularly when I am dealing with an uncomfortable sense of common humanity shared with women I have nothing else in common with, and I'm angry that I even feel it's an insult, Watson thinking I might be one of the sad, scarred women onstage. I flipped my PI license so that he could see it. "I was wondering how long you've been working here at the Bunkhouse."

He glanced at my license and my face. "Longer'n you've been alive is my guess. But if you're looking for somebody, I gotta warn you that I don't remember too well."

"I'm looking for a man who used to be a bartender here, a man named Danny O'Neal." I pulled a fifty out of my pocket. This would go on Mom's tab, too. "Maybe we could have a drink while you try to remember him."

Watson's small, wrinkled hand, with long fingers like a monkey's, closed over mine, gently pushing it away. "I don't want your money, kid. I'm an old man, and I told you, I don't remember too well."

He looked up at me earnestly, the lined face under the dark wig appearing as grotesque in its own way as the distorted breasts of the women onstage. I suddenly felt sorry for him, too.

"Okay." I tucked the fifty back in my pocket and took out

a business card. "If you want that drink sometime, even if you don't remember anything, give me a call."

"Yeah, sure." He turned back to the bar and the waiting shot glass. "Good luck, kid."

I left the card on the bar, next to his elbow.

The bouncer nodded good-bye and held the door as I walked out.

I had never been in the Bunkhouse before and was too tied into what was going on to reflect on anything while I was inside. So I was on the street looking back at the sign in the window, the sketched breasts with their huge pointed nipples, which somehow reminded me of the line of Freud's that everything is a penis symbol except the penis itself, which is a breast symbol, when the question hit me again: Why had Danny been working there? With all the bars in Reno, and all the years he had been a bartender, why was he working that freak show?

I hadn't thought I had any illusions left about Danny when I walked in there. I was certain I didn't have any when I walked out. A feeling was sneaking up from the back of my mind, one I was going to have to confront in the not-too-distant future, that not only had I not really known my father, I probably wouldn't have liked him if I had.

I was still staring at the sign when one of the smelly sport coats left the bar. I think it was the one whose finger I twisted, because he glanced at me and walked the other way. My only triumph of the evening, and a small one indeed.

Chapter
5

"OKAY, MOM, LET'S try one more time."

"You are not a prosecuting attorney, and I am not on trial." She was snapping at me again.

"I'm sorry. But you're just not being very helpful."

"This is far enough." She stopped walking, turned toward the water, and sat down on the closest rock.

Lying awake in bed the night before, I had decided that we had to talk in person, and so first thing in the morning, which meant about ten o'clock for me, I had driven up to Mom and Al's modest chalet at the north end of Lake Tahoe. Al was having some sort of campaign committee meeting in the living room, which was fine with me, because I had wanted to get Mom out of the house. The sky was a clear, icy blue, with the few high clouds over the indigo mountains only serving as a reminder of just how much space was up there. A slight breeze had raised a few rippling whitecaps on the lake, and a handful of sailboats crisscrossed one another's paths, leaning at what seemed impossible angles as they tacked.

Mom's beaded moccasins were really too fragile to walk any distance in, but we had come the half mile or so from the house to the beach, almost to the water, before she started complaining. We were close enough to a pile of boulders for her to find a low one and slip onto it, pulling her feet up after her. The breeze kept pushing red curls into her eyes, and she kept trying to brush them back. If I'd had an extra rubber band, I would have offered it.

I climbed around her to a boulder slightly higher and closer to the water and settled, letting my feet dangle over the edge, boots just out of reach of the lapping water. The day was lovely, cool enough to walk but warm enough to do it without a jacket, for me, if not for Mom. I wished we were up there for no other reason than to enjoy it. But we had to talk, something that had never worked very well for us.

"I need to know more about him, Mom. I need to know more about Danny, or I won't be able to find him. I'm not even sure where to look next." I looked out at the lake as I said it. I thought maybe it would be easier for her to answer if I didn't look at her. "The more I find out on my own, the less sense it makes to me. Remembering him, I can sort of imagine him at the Old Corral. But not at the Bunkhouse. And it isn't just that I don't like the idea of Danny working at the Bunkhouse. Reno was booming in the seventies—it wasn't as if bartender jobs were scarce, not for someone who knew as many people as Danny did. And there had to be a lot of places not just classier, but that would have paid better."

"I'm sorry. I'm afraid it's been too many years, and I can't remember a lot of things about Danny."

"Come on. You sound like a politician disclaiming a youthful attachment to Hitler." That was the wrong thing to say. "Okay. Forget the Bunkhouse. Tell me something else. Anything else. Tell me about meeting him, tell me why you married him. I don't care." When she didn't say anything, I added, "That's not true. I do care."

She still didn't say anything. I decided to watch sailboats

until she was ready to thaw a little. Al had been into sailing for a while, right after he retired, and I had gone out with them twice. Both times I was cold, wet, and sick. That wouldn't have made any difference, except that Mom was, too. Two of the few times that I ever felt close to her. Al sold the sailboat at the end of the summer. In fact, Mom's demand for comfort was the big thing I had going for me at the moment. Sooner or later she was going to want food, warmth, or indoor plumbing.

"We met in high school, you know that," she said, finally.

I think it was the breeze that got to her first. It was too early for her to want lunch, and she had used the bathroom before we left the house. I did know they had met in high school, but I wasn't going to help her out. I waited.

"Danny O'Neal wore a black leather jacket over a white T-shirt with rolled-up sleeves, all the time. And black peggers. I used to worry about how many white T-shirts he had, and how often he washed them. He had long hair—I thought it was long then—combed into a ducktail. A D.A. He looked like a blond Elvis."

I thought I heard her giggle, but I didn't turn around to check.

"I was so fascinated by him," she said, "but I couldn't let anyone know. Except one girlfriend, my best friend— Lynette Snow. I told Lynette I had a crush on Danny O'Neal, and she promised to keep it a secret, because she knew my mother would die if she found out. Danny and I didn't have any classes together, partly because he was a year ahead of me, but also because I was on the college prep track and Danny took vocational courses. I only saw him at lunch, but I knew he noticed me. One counselor might have caught us eyeing each other, because early in my junior year, when I was planning my senior class schedule with her and talking about the future, she changed the subject to a conversation about judging by appearances. She told me that I had one of the highest IQ scores in the school, but that I would never guess whose was right behind me, by only one point—Danny O'Neal's."

College prep tracks and IQ scores sounded like science fiction to me, even for Reno in the late fifties, and what the counselor said was a serious ethical breach. But it wasn't the moment to interrupt and tell her so.

"I lied to him," she continued. "I decided that was my opening, and I lied to him. I waited for him in the lunch line, and I told him our IQ scores were the same. He laughed, but he didn't move away, and we sat down at the same table. Nobody sat with us, but I knew everybody was staring. I was dy-ing."

She sounded so young and vulnerable that I was starting to get embarrassed. Besides, she hadn't lied. IQ tests aren't that accurate. For all practical purposes, their scores were the same. One point was only enough so that Mom would always believe she was smarter than Danny.

"He was waiting for me after school. I always walked home—we lived up the hill from the high school, not that far, and there was a shortcut through a vacant lot. He started walking with me, every day. But he would leave at the top of the hill, before the curve in the street, so no one would see us together." She paused. "You don't remember your grandparents very well, do you?"

"I don't remember Grandpa," I said. "Except as an angry old man, a dark cloud who waved a cane. I don't remember him as a person. I remember Grandma, a little. She was fat, and she held me on her lap and rocked me. And you made me go see her in the nursing home, when she was tied to the bed and didn't know who I was."

That was wrong, too. I was better off not talking at all, no matter what she said.

"I shouldn't have done that. I didn't realize how much it would upset you. And I thought she might know you, I thought it might help her." That was quiet, but then she shouted at me. "I didn't want to see her like that either, you know. It was hard for me, too."

The wind carried her words across the lake. I pulled my legs up and hugged my knees. I still didn't look at her. After a while, she started talking again.

"You don't know what it was like then," she said. "We barely had Tampax. Nobody knew anything about birth control, except that people who practiced the rhythm method were called parents. I couldn't talk to my mother about any of the things I was feeling, because nice girls didn't, and we were a middle-class family. Nice, all of us. I knew about passion, and I knew it could make fools of women, because I had read *Forever Amber*."

"You read what?" I couldn't help it. Not only did I blurt it out, I turned around to look at her.

"I read *Forever Amber*. A novel. About a woman who was the king's mistress and then lost everything because of her passion for a man who didn't love her." Mom was hugging her knees, too, and her normally porcelain skin was blotched. She looked young and puzzled.

"You got involved with Danny because of a cheap historical novel? That's worse than Elvis!"

"Don't judge me! I was only seventeen!" Her spine straightened, and I was afraid I had destroyed the fragile bond of the day. But she started talking again. "And it wasn't because of a book that I fell in love with Danny. It was because he seemed dangerous and exciting and forbidden. And anything but middle-class nice. I would tell my mother that I was going to the movies with Lynette, and I would, but Danny would meet us there, and I would sit with him, holding hands at first, then making out. My whole life became centered around Saturdays, around making out with Danny at the movies. Lynette would tell me afterward what the movie was about, so I could tell my mother when I got home. Then we started making out after school, too. Not for very long, because I had to get home before my mother suspected. I don't remember how many weeks this went on. I do remember the first time he asked me to meet him somewhere else, not the movies, and I knew it was so that we could go all the way."

The expression was quaint, but there was something touching about it, imagining a seventeen-year-old Mom, and what the thrill of going "all the way" with her bad boy lover would be.

"Where did you go?" I asked.

She stared out at the water for a long time. "Danny worked occasionally for a friend with a motorcycle repair shop. It was closed Sundays. That weekend I said that Lynette and I were going to the movies on Sunday, not Saturday, because a Jimmy Stewart festival was opening at the Crest Theater on Sunday. The movie was *Broken Arrow*. I rented the videotape years later, and I cried all the way through."

"Oh, hell, Mom. That's the one where he falls in love with the Indian girl and she's killed. Everybody cries in that one."

"Do you want to hear this story or not?" she snapped.

"I'm sorry. I do want to hear it."

"The office was at the back of an asphalt yard littered with partly decomposed motorcycles. It was surrounded by a chain-link fence—Danny had the key to the padlock—and guarded by a pit bull who was so excited that Danny showed up on a Sunday that he kept running around the yard, wriggling and barking, and coming over so that Danny could pet him, and then running away again. The office was just this filthy shed, really, with a desk and a filing cabinet and an old army cot instead of a sofa. Danny had brought a bottle of cheap wine in a brown paper bag, and there were Dixie cups in a dispenser next to a water cooler. We were both nervous, and neither one of us knew anything about sex, and the dog kept barking because he was shut outside and he wanted Danny to pay attention to him, and it was terrible."

She was silent again, and when I turned to see what she was doing, she was all huddled up on the rock, not even brushing the hair out of her face.

"I'm sorry, Mom," I said again. "Really I am. I'm sorry it wasn't better." I'm not good at offering comfort under any circumstances. Trying to find words to comfort my mother because she lost her virginity under lousy conditions was impossible.

"Well, it couldn't have been, could it?" She lifted her head and stared, wild-eyed. "How could it have been any good? Week after week we met there, and it was never any good, because we were too young to know what good was. The first time it was good was an accident, after the baby died."

"What?"

"You almost had an older brother. That's why Danny and I got married. I tried to deny it as long as I could, but I got pregnant within a month. By then it was almost the end of the school year, and I was frantic, not knowing how I would get to see Danny. He was graduating, and he was going to be working full-time at the motorcycle shop. I had a summer job at a stationery shop. I personalized notepaper and envelopes with a machine that stamped the names and addresses through foil."

I almost interrupted on that one, but I didn't.

"And Lynette was going on vacation with her parents, so

I couldn't use the movies as a cover for the whole month of June. By the end of June I was hysterical. My period was so late that I was certain I was pregnant, and I started feeling sick when I woke up in the morning, and I didn't know what to do. One day I couldn't stand it any longer, so I told the woman I worked for that I was sick, and I had to go home. She said I looked terrible, and she wanted to call my mother. I just ran out. I walked all the way to the motorcycle shop, it seemed like miles. Danny was so glad to see me—even the pit bull was glad to see me. Danny was all covered with grease, his white T-shirt was filthy, but I hugged him anyway. I was wearing a blue and white striped cotton blouse, and a matching circle skirt, and the grease stains never did come out. I told him I had to talk to him—I thought I might be p.g.—and he yelled at his boss that he had to take the rest of the day off. He had a motorcycle by then, and I pulled my skirt up so I could sit behind him. We went to the Wigwam coffee shop, and he bought us both some hot apple pie with vanilla sauce, and cherry Cokes. And he said he wanted to marry me."

Mom was more than blotchy. She had started to cry. I would have looked away, but she was speaking so quietly that if I hadn't faced her, I would have lost the words. And I knew this was my only shot. She had never told me this story before, and she wouldn't tell it again.

"We drove to my house on the motorcycle and told my mother. She didn't take it well. She wailed and she sobbed and we thought she was going to collapse. She didn't, of course. You don't remember, I know, but fragile was part of her act."

She was wrong—that was one of the few things I did remember about Grandma. Always using a weak heart as an excuse for not being able to do anything for herself.

"Eventually, she agreed to pay for the marriage, a small

ceremony, at home, just a few friends. That would have been the right choice anyway, because Danny's mother was dying of cancer, and a big wedding wouldn't have been appropriate."

"Jesus. A good time was had by all."

She mustered an almost laugh. "It got worse. We moved in with his mother, sleeping in Danny's room in a dreadful little two-bedroom tract house in Sparks. She died, and I miscarried at seven months. Right at Christmas. Now they save preemies, but they couldn't then. I cried at Christmas for years after that."

"I wish you'd told me. I never understood why everybody else looked forward to Christmas, and ours were always so silent and miserable, even when Danny was still around."

"Well, I probably should have told you. But there was never a good moment."

Somehow that struck both of us as funny. Mom wiped her tears and tried again to brush the curls out of her face. The breeze pushed them back.

"How did you and Danny survive the first year? Why didn't you break up then?"

"Because I couldn't go home and say I'd made a mistake. And besides, that was when the sex finally started being good, when the two of us were there alone, playing out some kind of teenage fantasy of the American dream. Danny worked at the motorcycle shop and I kept house. I had to finish high school at night, the adult school, because I was married. It took a while, but I got pregnant again, with you."

"What went wrong? Why don't I remember you two happy together?"

"Oh, hell, I don't know. Danny's mother had left us a little money along with her equity in the house, not much, and when that was gone, Danny had to get a second job. He was twenty-one by then, and he got a night job as a bartender. I'm not sure when that became his first job. I was taking care of you, and I never got out, and I never got to see anybody except my mother, who would come over every once in a while to take me to lunch. Danny and I spent the holidays with them, but my father didn't like Danny, never got over my marrying a bum—which was how he saw Danny, rightly or not—and he was always rude. Lynette stopped by to see me for a while, but when she started college and pledged a sorority, our lives were so different that she stopped."

"Why didn't you go to college?"

"Because there didn't seem to be any point. I was married, and I didn't plan on working, and I think I felt it would be hitting Danny over the head with the fact that I was smarter than he was."

One IQ point.

"Your aunt Rickie sent letters sometimes, always telling me I ought to get a job, but I thought I ought to stay home with you."

Aunt Rickie—Frederica—was Mom's older sister, for whom I was named. She had come through Reno a couple of times, always from someplace different, always with a different husband. I never got to know my cousins. And I winced at Mom's admission that she saw staying home as a duty, not a choice.

"When Danny joined the Marines—he did it on impulse, after a fight, the way he did so many things—and then he was sent to Vietnam, and I had to get a job with the telephone company, I think in some ways it was a relief. And even though we stayed together for five years after he got back, we never really connected again." She stood up and stretched, arms out straight, and I realized she was through with the story. Then she hugged herself. "Do you

want to start back? I should have worn a heavier jacket. I
don't want to interrupt Al's meeting, but we could have a
cup of coffee in the kitchen. And if you want to wait until
the meeting's over, we can all go to the Cal-Neva for
lunch."

"I'll take the coffee. I think I'll skip lunch."

She stepped down from the rock she was sitting on and
waited for me on the sand. She was wearing a white denim
jacket over a deep mustard cashmere sweater, and she
looked cold, but she still looked young. We trudged up
toward the highway—or I trudged, boots sinking in the fine,
soft sand, while she walked lightly. After we crossed the
road and started up the trail through the tall pines, out of the
sun, the temperature dropped ten degrees. Coffee was a
good idea.

Half a dozen cars parked on the gravel outside the
two-story cedar log house were a good indication that the
meeting was still in progress. They had been there when I
arrived, so I had left the Jeep a few yards down the road. We
slipped between the cars, entered quietly, and moved
directly into the small, cheerful kitchen. The coffeemaker
was on, but down to less than a cup. Mom dumped it and
started a new pot. I leaned against the stove.

"What about friends?" I asked. "Why didn't you know
any of Danny's friends except Sam?"

"For the first few years we were married, Danny occasionally tried to bring a friend home, or we would go to a
party given by one of his friends. I didn't like the men and
I was horrified by their wives—stupid women, all of them,
who were trampled by their husbands. I suppose I was
horrified because I was afraid of becoming one of them.
When he started working two jobs, he didn't try any longer.
Sam was the only one who was ever in the house after that.
Every once in a while he would show up on his bike and

sleep on the living-room couch. It didn't seem to bother him that I didn't much like him. He'd go out of his way to be nice to me—I think because he could see how unhappy I was."

She stopped again and got coffee mugs from the cupboard next to the sink. She filled one and handed it to me, then her own.

I held the mug, letting it warm my hands.

"One more thing. The Bunkhouse."

"I told you, I don't remember." She got tense, then relented a little. "Danny always had a get-rich-quick scheme. Working at the Bunkhouse may have been connected to one of them, or maybe the Bunkhouse was the only place that would hire him. His stupid schemes never worked, and he would have done a lot better if he had just taken a job at one of the clubs and stayed. But he lost his job at Harrah's after they caught him counting cards at twenty-one, and of course the word spread."

Counting cards used to be a way for somebody with a good memory to beat the house, but it only worked with a single deck. For a while, the clubs barred counters from playing. Now the twenty-one dealers use shoes with multiple decks, and the counters are simply out of luck.

"Did he really think he was going to get rich counting cards?"

"Absolutely he did. He poured from the well and charged for brand, too. Stupid and petty!" she snapped.

Next she was going to accuse him of bad taste.

I could remember lying awake in bed, listening to them, listening to her, really, yelling at him. I'd always thought it was because of the other women. But this made more sense to me—and it helped make sense out of the feeling I'd had that other women were his way of getting even with her for something. Mom had never believed in Danny, probably rightly—just like her father—but that must have been a killer for him.

"What are you thinking?" she asked. "You think it's my fault he left, don't you?"

"No. I used to blame you, when I didn't blame me, but now I think it's probably a lot more complicated." The thought of Danny and get-rich-quick schemes needed more attention. I was going to have to get away from Mom, though. "This is probably a silly question, since you said you didn't know any of his friends. Did Danny ever mention a Gary Hanrahan?"

"The name sounds vaguely familiar. Wasn't Hanrahan one of the old Irish heroes or something like that?"

"I don't know. Probably. It sounds like a name Yeats would use in a poem."

"Why do you want to know?"

"Because he's dead. I asked him about Danny, and then somebody shot him. And I don't know whether there's any connection."

"Oh, dear God!" She put down her coffee mug on the kitchen counter, and she was suddenly middle-aged and blotchy again. "This wasn't a good idea, was it, trying to find Danny."

"Why not? What's wrong?"

"Nothing. Except that I hadn't realized it might be dangerous."

"Come on, Mom. Getting out of bed can be dangerous. Taking showers can be dangerous. So—did you know Gary Hanrahan?"

"No." She said it firmly. "No. I didn't know Gary Hanrahan."

The noises from the living room had been building, and now people were moving toward the front door, a path that would take them right by the entrance to the kitchen. Heads were leaning in to say good-bye to Mom. She put on her smile mask and charmed them. I tried to be invisible so that she wouldn't feel she had to introduce me to anybody. Cars started, one at a time. Al shut the door behind the last person.

"How did it go?" Mom asked with forced cheer.

"I am cautiously optimistic," he answered, coming into the kitchen. His smile faded when he saw me. "Hello, Freddie."

"Hi, Al."

Al is big and heavyset, if not quite fat, and he took up a lot of the kitchen. The few gray hairs on top of his head were standing on end, as if he'd been rubbing his scalp. He did that sometimes when he talked seriously.

"Coming with us for lunch? I know Ramona'd love to have you join us."

"No, thanks. I gotta get back." I slid past Mom to leave my coffee mug in the sink. "Thanks for thinking of me, though."

Mom caught my arm and hugged it. "Please don't do anything more dangerous than taking a shower."

I turned and hugged her back. I'm always surprised at how small she is.

"I promise."

Al moved away from the doorway so that I could get out, and we expressed the proper sentiments as I left.

I walked down to the Jeep, used the driveway to turn around, negotiated the narrow road down to Highway 28, and turned left, following the shimmering lake back toward Highway 50. Time to put the top on, especially if I was going to be coming up to see Mom occasionally. I was hungry, as well as cold, and almost wished I had tolerated Al through lunch.

That brought up one question I hadn't asked, something that had always bothered me. If Mom had all that time on her hands, with nothing to do except take care of me and a small house, why the hell hadn't she ever learned to cook?

Chapter
6

THOSE OF US who are self-employed, with offices in our homes, and without significant relationships, live differently from the rest of the civilized world. The up side is that we get up and go to bed when we feel like it, work when the work is there, and never have to think about food because someone else is hungry. The down side is that we sometimes forget the patterns that most other people cut for their lives. In this case, when I drove out to the Old Corral that evening to talk with Hardy McCullen or anyone else who might be there about Gary Hanrahan, I forgot until I saw the filled parking lot that it was Friday, and Friday is a heavy drinking night for the Old Corral's clientele. A heavy date night, too, as I discovered when I tried to work my way to the bar.

While I had planned to leave Hanrahan's murder to Maddox, unless I ran into something that definitely tied it to Danny, I got restless when I realized that I didn't have much in the way of leads to pursue, and I wasn't quite ready to walk the streets of Las Vegas looking for Jackie Ellis. So when a workout with the weights I keep in my living room (what was meant to be the second bedroom, since the official living room is my office) didn't help, and I couldn't concentrate well enough even to beat the computer at Scrabble, I fed the cats, grabbed my jacket, and left.

I thought about walking to the Mother Lode and looking for Deke, but I didn't have anything to say to him, and I didn't want his advice. I wanted to feel I was doing something at least marginally useful. So I thought of the Old Corral. I picked up a drive-thru hamburger and ate it on the way to the bar, just to have something in my stomach to absorb the beer.

The music on Friday and Saturday didn't come from a jukebox. The lights were up on the stage, where a man with an electric guitar wailed about his lost love, backed by a second guitar, bass, and drums. All four men were dressed in western-gone-glitter, with cigarette-leg pants tucked into the kind of stitched, hand-painted cowboy boots that were never meant to be exposed to barnyard mud, or horseshit, or any of the things that real boots are designed to weather.

The dance floor was crowded with couples, a few men and a lot of women dressed in the same kind of glitter, most of the men wearing work shirts, Levi's, and boots that understood what they were supposed to be. The tables seemed crowded, too, and I couldn't figure out how the room was going to absorb the dancers when the music ended.

McCullen was working the end of the bar farthest from the bandstand, the end that included the space for the servers, which on that night were two ponytailed women wearing cutoffs and tank tops who looked so young they would have had their IDs checked if they hadn't been waiting tables. A thin blond man who looked marginally older than the servers was holding down the other end of the bar. No sign of Farrell.

McCullen nodded when he saw me. "Draft?"

"Yeah, thanks." I was leaning sideways between two

six-footers in denim jackets wearing hats, who almost made me feel short. Almost. "Do you take a break?"

"For you, anytime," he said with a grin. He pulled the beer and slapped the glass on a napkin in front of me. "Except that I have to wait for Cliff. He takes over for an hour, usually about ten, so that Strider and I get breaks."

"Strider? That blond kid is named Strider?"

"Strider Smith. His mother read Tolkien at an impressionable age, what can I tell you. Gotta go."

Life could have been worse. Mom could have named me Amber.

I had arrived a little after nine. Farrell showed up about halfway through my second beer, not long before the band decided to take a break. He noted my presence, although he didn't say anything.

There was a rush for the bar as the dance floor cleared, and I realized the tables didn't accommodate everyone. The place was a fire marshal's nightmare. Farrell lifted a section of the counter and stepped behind the bar, helped out until the first round of orders was taken care of, and then whispered something to McCullen. McCullen nodded, wiped his hands, and ducked through the still-lifted section of counter, closing it afterward. I extricated myself from my niche and elbowed toward him.

"Come on," he said. "We'll sit in the office."

I followed him down the length of the bar. We turned at the arrow to the rest rooms, but he opened the door next to the one labeled "Stallions," one with a sign that said simply "Office." I looked at the third sign, on the other side of the wall. Mares. It would be snowing in July before I'd walk through a door labeled "Mares." I would have to remember not to drink too much beer.

The office was one of the few I've seen that was more cluttered than mine. The problem was that there was barely room for the desk, the filing cabinet, and an extra chair. McCullen sat on the edge of the desk, and I took the side chair. He waited for me to say something, his good eye focused on me, the other one off to my left somewhere.

"Has Maddox been back?" I asked.

"Yeah, he was here last night, questioning the regulars."

"Did they talk after he left?"

"Couldn't have shut 'em up if I'd wanted to. None of 'em gave half a damn about Gary while he was alive, but once he was murdered, he was everybody's best buddy. Everybody had a story to tell."

"I don't suppose any of the stories were about who might have wanted to kill Hanrahan."

"Not one."

"And I don't suppose anybody knew where he was coming from when he was shot."

"Right again. One more and you win a free beer."

I had to do it. "I don't suppose Maddox dropped any clues about anything else he'd found out."

McCullen laughed. "The beer's on the house."

"Thanks."

"You said you were going to stay out of this, unless you found a reason to tie Hanrahan's murder to your father. Did you?"

"Oh, hell. No. I just needed someplace to go and ask questions tonight."

"Got any more?"

I was about to say no, but I decided to try a long shot. "One. Do you know of any connection between the Old Corral and the Bunkhouse?"

"Not now." He frowned. "But it seems to me that Tommy Farrell, Cliff's brother, used to own the Bunkhouse."

"Why are you frowning? What's the story?"

"You'll have to ask Cliff, or somebody who's been

around longer than I have. In fact, Gary Hanrahan probably would have been a good person to ask. Tommy Farrell was murdered, years ago, and I think it was at the Bunkhouse."

I started to ask another question, but he stopped me.

"I don't know any of the details," he said. "I don't know the year, even."

"You must know something—like whether the murderer was ever caught, for example."

McCullen's bad eye was jumping like crazy. "Not even that, although it seems to me he wasn't. Listen, do me a favor and don't ask Cliff about it, at least not tonight. He knows we're talking, and he'll know I told you, and I don't want any static from him. I don't think he'd like my talking about his family business."

"Shit. Okay. I didn't want to stay any longer anyway." One more beer and I'd have to use the door marked "Mares."

"Here." McCullen picked up a pencil and scribbled something on a piece of paper. "My phone number. You don't have to drive all the way out here just for one or two questions."

"Thanks. I appreciate that."

He smiled, and this time it just seemed friendly, not so wolflike. He hopped off the desk and opened the office door, holding it for me. I hate it when men do that, but I let it go.

The band was playing again, and this time the wail was about the singer's dead mother. I couldn't figure out why so many people wanted to dance to a song about a dead mother. I edged my way around the dance floor and out of the building.

I hadn't realized how hot it had been inside until I was hit by the chill. I wished I had worn my sheepskin jacket, instead of the denim. The heater in the Jeep worked fine, but with the top off, a lot of the warm air dissipated. I turned it up high and moved it to defrost, so at least some of the heat would get to my face.

I slowed down as I passed the curve where I had found Hanrahan. If it hadn't been so cold, I would have stopped, not because I thought I'd find anything, just because it might have helped me think. I needed to find out when Tommy Farrell had been murdered, so that I could look up the reports. I didn't want to jump to any conclusions here. Besides, if Cliff Farrell thought Danny had murdered his brother . . . No. He wouldn't have told me so. He would probably have behaved just about the way he had, just that cool.

There was one other person I had talked with who had been around as long as Gary Hanrahan. Ev Watson, at the Bunkhouse. I didn't want to go back there, but it was the fastest way I could think of to get the information, short of asking Farrell. I was annoyed that McCullen had asked me not to, although I could see why he wouldn't want to get caught gossiping about his boss's murdered brother.

By the time I had driven the few miles back to Reno, I was shivering. I stopped at my house, turned the heat on, microwaved some instant coffee, and stood in front of a vent as I drank it. There was a black stain on the wall, where the oily smoke from the furnace had paused on its way into the air I breathe. As soon as I got a little ahead, I would have to buy a new furnace, one that didn't burn oil. Some fuel less expensive and better for the environment. My lungs, as well.

I finished the coffee and rummaged in the closet until I found my sheepskin jacket. I don't have that many clothes, but I have games and books and the overflow of the detritus from the living-room closet in there, and since I never get around to sorting, things are always hard to find unless I've used them recently.

The coffee and the jacket were sufficient fortification

against the night cold that I took the time to put the top on the Jeep. It didn't take long, but doing it allowed me to postpone the Bunkhouse for a few more minutes.

I drove the mile or so to the Bunkhouse, and then had to face again the reality of Friday night crowds, which meant parking the car around the corner and walking back. I kept my head down, so I wouldn't have to look at the sign with the volcano tits.

The bouncer remembered me. "You really want to see the show again?"

"No. But it's the only way I know how to talk with Ev Watson tonight. When is the break?"

"About twenty minutes. But there's no room. We're full up."

"Hell. I don't want to stand here in the cold for twenty minutes."

"No, I expect you don't. Why don't you wait in the lobby? You'll know when the show's over, you'll hear the applause."

"The lobby?"

He smiled, showing two gold-capped front teeth. "I suppose it ain't exactly a lobby, but it's where they go into the hotel."

I opened the other door to the building, the one that led to the stairs. If there was any kind of registration desk, it had to be on the second floor. I didn't go up to find out. Instead, I leaned against the wall, listening for sounds of applause, wishing I understood what determines who gets applause and who doesn't in this world.

The wall was thin, and I could pick up the vibration of the drum that kept the rhythm for the last act. It must have been hell for anybody in a room above the stage. Finally, a roll signaled the moment when the stripper ended her act with a high kick that broke her G-string, exposing her shaved genitalia to the audience. The guys love it. I waited for the applause to end and counted to sixty after that, giving Watson time to get to the bar. When I stepped back out onto the sidewalk, it was milling with men. A couple of them looked at me questioningly, but I headed straight for the door and the bouncer. He moved forward enough that I could slip behind him into the still-crowded room.

Watson had made it within leaning distance of the bar. In fact, he had downed one shot and had his hand out for another when I tapped his shoulder. He glanced at me, back at the glass, and took one sip.

"I told you I can't remember your father," he said.

"I don't remember telling you he was my father."

"I picked up your card after you left. I'm old, but I'm not stupid."

"Sorry. Anyway, I'm not asking about him tonight. I'm asking about Tommy Farrell's murder."

One swallow took care of the rest of the shot.

"Oh, hell, honey, don't do this. I told you, my memory's no good."

"Just give me a date. Please. I'll look up the rest in the newspapers. I can find out anyway—I can look up the records on the Bunkhouse, see who owns it, when it was last sold, and work from there. But it'll be faster if you tell me. Please."

He held out his glass to the bartender for a refill.

"Follow me."

He balanced the glass carefully, not quite at the length of his short arm, as he worked his way through the mostly new crowd pushing to find seats.

I followed him behind the dusty curtain, across the narrow stage, into a cold, cement-floored area with two doors leading out. I could hear loud chatter behind one. He opened the other, and we entered a small room that held a table with a makeup kit, one chair, and a coat rack.

"My dressing room," he said, gesturing grandly. "Twenty-two years here, and this is home. Take the chair."

"It's okay. I'll stand."

"Please sit. I'm not comfortable looking that far up. I'll get a crick in my neck."

I sat, wishing I could offer the smile he so obviously wanted. He took a sip from his shot glass, carefully, as if he wanted this one to last.

"I really meant it," he said, round-eyed and wrinkled under the full brown wig. "I don't remember when Tommy Farrell was murdered."

"Maybe not. But you could tell me whether it was before or after Danny O'Neal split town."

"Not even that, for sure. Danny had gone from here to the Old Corral, and then I heard from somebody that he wasn't a bartender any longer. I think that was about the time Farrell was murdered, but it was all a long time ago. What I want to say to you is, you're off on the wrong track if you're trying to connect your father to Farrell's murder, or anybody else's. Danny was a good-looking, lighthearted guy who liked whiskey and women and small scams, not necessarily in that order. He wasn't a murderer. I wouldn't ever believe that." Watson took another small sip. "Farrell was killed upstairs here, in bed with a hooker. Somebody with a shotgun, got her, too. No witnesses. Nobody ever charged. Certainly nothing that would tie Danny to the crime. He didn't even work here then. I know you don't want any advice, but I'm going to give it anyway. When somebody wants to disappear, you got to let them go. You're listed in the telephone directory, Danny could find you. If he hasn't, it's because he doesn't want to. Why he left, where he is now, none of that matters. Or it shouldn't. Just let him stay lost, kid. Do something else with your life."

I was getting tense and angry listening to him, angry that he was giving advice—he was right, I didn't want it—but angrier that this pathetic old man had known my father better than I did.

"I'll think about what you said." I stood, holding out my hand. "And thanks for the information."

"But not for the advice, I know." He placed his limp paw in my hand. "I hope you take care of yourself, kid."

I left him there to prepare for the next show, whatever that meant. I hurried through the cold backstage area and across the tiny stage, almost tripping over a stagehand standing ready to open the curtain, who glared at me. The barroom was full again, with the same low murmur that had anticipated the show the first night I had been there.

"Get what you wanted?" the bouncer asked.

"Close enough. Thanks for letting me in."

"No problem," he said, holding the door to let me out.

I walked toward my car with my head down against the cold. I didn't think it was freezing, but the temperature had surely dropped to the mid-thirties, cooler than usual for late September in Reno. I tried to feel for a hunch, whether Danny was connected with the Farrell murder or not, but my anger—anger at Watson, but even more, anger at Danny, for leaving in the first place—got in the way. So at first I didn't notice that someone had fallen into step beside me.

"Looks like we're heading in the same direction," a man's voice said, followed by a funny snuffling sound.

"We're not," I answered, without looking up. "Fuck off."

Dealing with men on the prowl is not something I like to do when I'm feeling at peace with the world. But I was almost relieved to be presented with a good outlet for my rage.

"No need to get testy. It's cold, let's find someplace warm, and I'll buy you a drink." Same snuffle.

"Hey—can't you hear? Are you some kind of dummy? I'll say it again! Fuck off!" I stopped and turned to face him. He was about my height, wearing a maroon parka zipped up to his chin, and a stocking cap pulled down over his ears. The snuffling sound was evidently the way he breathed through a nose so lumpy it was a wonder he could breathe at all. But it was the eyes that got me. They were dark and vacant. If I had looked at those eyes first, I would have been more careful what I said to him. I backpedaled as best I could. "Look, I'm on my way to meet a friend. I'm in a hurry. He's waiting for me. No offense."

"None taken." Snuffle. "But maybe your friend won't mind if you're a little late."

"He would mind. He has a short temper. But I'll tell you what—I'll walk with you as far as the Bunkhouse. I'll bet you can find someone to drink with there, someone a lot more fun than I am." I hated myself for what I was doing. I reminded myself of my mother—do anything to survive. I started to edge back the way I had come, but he stepped in my way.

"I saw you come out of the Bunkhouse."

Shit.

"I was just in there talking to Ev Watson, the comic. He's an old friend of my father's." Keeping it close to the truth might help.

"Maybe I'm an old friend of your father's, too."

"Funny, he never mentioned you."

He laughed, somewhere between a snuffle and a snort, but it didn't ease the tension.

"That's good. But maybe he just forgot to mention me. You don't know, do you? Maybe he was in jail, and didn't tell you. Maybe I knew him in prison. What do you think of that?"

I thought that struck a nerve. "Hey, maybe you're right," was what I said. "I'll tell you what, let's go back to the Bunkhouse, and you can buy me that drink and tell me about it."

"No. Let's go to your house."

Fear trumps anger. The heat of rage had been washed away by an icy awareness that this man could hurt me. And enjoy it. I tried to remember whether I was supposed to be better off looking him in the eye, to show I wasn't afraid, or looking away, to show I wasn't challenging him. I stayed with his eyes, figuring they would alert me to any sudden moves.

"That's not a good idea," I said, concentrating on keeping my voice low and calm. "I told you, someone is expecting me."

"We'll surprise him."

"No."

"Yes."

I didn't see it coming. He slammed me against the building with his right hand around my throat and his right knee between my thighs. The smell of his body was enough to choke me.

"I wanted to be nice to you," he said. "But if you want it rough, we can play it that way."

My hands had been in my pockets when he stopped me, and my left hand came out with my car keys in them, aiming for his eyes. He had to jerk his head away, but his grip didn't loosen. I stomped on his left instep, full strength. He had to take his right knee away to get his balance. I brought my left forearm under and around, against his wrist, but his hand closed tighter on my throat. He grabbed my arm with his left hand, and I smacked his ear with my right fist.

He hadn't expected me to fight. His grip on my throat eased enough for me to get a deep breath and yell, *"No!"* At the same time I brought my right knee up, trying for his balls. I missed, but I hit the fleshy part of his stomach. He grunted. I aimed for his kneecap with the reinforced toe of my boot just as he slammed me on the side of the head.

The back of my head hit the wall, and for a moment I was afraid I was going to pass out. But I managed one more *"No!"* as I stomped his instep again.

I had a sense that lights were coming on, and I wasn't certain whether they were on the street or in my head. In either case, he let go of my throat, and I slid to the sidewalk. I sat there, dazed and shivering, until I felt a hand on my shoulder.

"You okay?"

It was the bouncer from the Bunkhouse.

"Give me a minute."

"Sure. Take your time. You need an ambulance?"

"Hell, no." I took his hand and let him pull me up.

"I told you you were on your own if anybody hit on you. For the record, you did good."

"Thanks. I don't suppose you know a vacant-eyed guy who snuffles when he breathes."

The bouncer laughed. "I see twenty a night. And I didn't get a good look at this one. You want to come back to the bar, have a drink, calm down a little?"

"No. I want to go home."

Our eyes locked and he nodded.

"I'll just watch from here until your car is started."

"Thanks again. How about walking me to the corner and watching from there?" If the guy came back, I knew he was going to be more trouble than I could handle alone.

He nodded again. "You got it."

The Jeep started, and nobody followed me home. I was glad I had left the heat on.

Butch and Sundance had evidently fought over my sweatshirt, because they were asleep on the bed with it bunched up between them. I checked the doors and windows, got rid of my clothes, and crawled into the space the cats had left for me.

I shivered for a while, but I went to sleep.

Chapter

7

"IF YOU SO much as think about going back to that place at night without me, you'll have more than a headache to worry about!" Deke's knife bounced against the plate, missed the edge, flipped to the counter, and clattered to the floor. "Diane!"

"Here's a clean knife, Deke," Diane said cheerfully. She had just refilled his coffee cup and was so close the roar nearly blew her over. "Try holding on to this one."

I had awakened on Saturday with a headache that was serious enough for me to stay home for the weekend, just in case I had a concussion from having my head slammed against a brick wall. I wasn't seeing double, but if I hadn't felt well enough to walk down to the Mother Lode for dinner on Sunday, I would have considered checking myself into Washoe Medical on Monday for a professional opinion.

Deke had been waiting in the coffee shop, furious before I even started talking because I hadn't been in all week to let him know what was going on. He wasn't any happier when he found out.

"I didn't expect any trouble," I said. The words sounded lame. "I didn't expect to be attacked by a psycho. Usually they prey on women who seem vulnerable."

"And you figured anybody could take one look and know you were wearing steel-tipped boots."

"Maybe not that, but certainly that I wouldn't go down without a fight."

"Suppose he wanted a fight? Suppose somebody paid him to want a fight?"

I put my half-eaten hamburger back on the plate. The possibility—remote as it was—that the guy hadn't picked me at random was enough to kill my appetite. It was his remark about my father. I couldn't help wondering if he knew something.

"I think the guy just figured anybody who was in the Bunkhouse had to be fair game."

"An assumption which is probably shared by half the men in Reno. And that is why you are not going back there alone." Deke followed a large bite of steak with a forkful of fries. This time, the knife stayed where he put it.

"Right now I don't see any reason to go back there at all. Watson is the only person who's been around long enough to remember anything, and he doesn't want to be helpful."

"You don't think the Farrell murder will take you back again?"

I stopped to watch the Keno board light up before I answered. Two of my numbers came up, not even enough to get my money back. I pulled out a dollar to replay the ticket.

"I don't think I'm smart enough to solve a fifteen-year-old murder."

"You aren't even smart enough to save your money, instead of dropping it on Keno. But you think you're smart enough to solve a new murder, like Gary Hanrahan's, especially if you think it'll take you in a direction you want to go, like toward finding Danny O'Neal. And if you stumble into a link between Hanrahan and Farrell along the way, you'll be right back at the Bunkhouse."

"Okay. You're right."

"Telling me I'm right ain't enough. I want you to promise that you won't go there alone again."

I had to think about what I was willing to promise. I don't like to break promises if I can help it.

"I promise to do my best to avoid dangerous situations, and to call you if I think I need backup."

Deke glowered at me through small, red-rimmed eyes that were almost swallowed by his heavy cheeks. "I suppose that's the best you can do."

"Yep." I picked up my hamburger, wasn't sure I wanted it, and put it back. But a couple of fries that had gone limp from too much ketchup went down all right, and I decided I was still hungry.

"You oughta get your head examined."

"It's better tonight. The pain's gone, and I don't think I had a concussion."

"It's the inside needs looking at. You don't always remember what friends are for, which is to help. And you don't remember that your friends care about you, and they want to help, and that's why they get mad when you don't care enough about them to ask for help when you should."

"Point made, Deke. I promise to remember."

I finished my hamburger, lost again at Keno, and declined Deke's offer to walk me home. I walked the few blocks between my house and the Mother Lode too often to allow fear to affect the trip, and having Deke walk with me would be like saying I was scared, and saying it might make it true. Beside, I truly didn't believe that the attack was anything other than random, and walking home alone was like getting back in the car and driving after an accident, something I had to do. The psycho's line about my father was just a random, lucky shot. Lucky for him, that is. The possibility that Danny had spent at least part of the time in jail was something I couldn't rule out. In a way, I almost wanted it to be true. It would make sense that he never got in touch if he was ashamed, if he didn't want to let me know he had been in jail.

The last two blocks down Mill Street I was conscious of how quiet it was. But again, nobody followed me home. The house was warm, and the cats were glad to see me. It was too cold for me to walk the block out of my way to the video store, even though I was edgy enough that I knew it was going to be late movie time. Fortunately, one of my favorites was on—Ray Milland and Marlene Dietrich in *Golden Earrings*, where Milland is a spy who pretends to be a gypsy and then learns to love the life. The ending had always seemed improbable before.

I fell asleep wondering if Danny had learned to love being on the run, if despite what he said to Sam and Moira, he realized that he had been running too long, and he had to keep going. I woke up in the night thinking about Sam and Moira and Doc, and I had some kind of revelation that I couldn't remember in the morning. Just as well. I had a lot to do.

I started at City Hall, one of those wonderful old buildings whose presence reminds you that Reno was once a frontier town, looking up records for the Bunkhouse. Normally, I would have walked to Stewart Street, especially since the day was that combination of cool, crisp, and still sunny that makes walking in the autumn a joy. Leaves were turning—I'm always surprised at how many deciduous trees there are in Reno, when the leaves turn briefly gold in the autumn. Almost immediately they turn brown and fall and the whole area looks gray and depressed until snow falls, but the short autumn, and the Indian summer that frequently marks it, are worth pausing for, worth breathing in. Still, I took the Jeep, because I wasn't certain how much running around I'd be doing.

I found a parking place on Lake Street, just around the corner, walked up the stairs to the entrance of the building, then down the stairs to the Recorder's Office. A thin man with sparse, sandy hair, wearing rimless bifocals, helped me find the right book and then the right page. The current owner of the Bunkhouse was one Roger Dayton, who had bought the place in 1981.

"It must have taken all that time for the estate to go through probate and the Farrells to find a buyer," the man commented.

"What do you mean?"

"You're too young to remember, but when Tommy Farrell, the former owner, was murdered, it was quite a story."

"Is that true, sir?" I said with all the innocence I could muster. "What happened?"

"I really don't know any more than I read in the papers— then there were two, it was before the *Examiner* folded, and the *Herald* became the survivor. But it was right around Christmas, 1977, when someone killed Tommy Farrell and the prostitute he was with. She was evidently one of the girls who lived at the Bunkhouse. Prostitution wasn't legal in Washoe County, of course, and the Bunkhouse was due for a raid anyway. The police closed the place, although I don't think they would have had many clients after the murder." He tittered, and I smiled politely.

The county-by-county choice on the legality of prostitution seemed to me one of the truly stupid state laws. It allowed one whoremaster to operate legally out of trailers at the edge of the county for years, just moving across the line when the sheriff showed up and moving back after he left.

"Why do you remember the year?" I asked.

"My wife was dying, and I sat with her in the hospital and read the newspapers to her every day, and talked to her as if she could hear me. The Farrell murder was one of the stories I read to her."

"I'm sorry." I hate it when people tell me those things. I don't know how to comfort them, and I never handle it well.

"It's all right, it's been a long time now. But that's why I remember the year." He smiled, and I was relieved that he wasn't still sad about it.

"Thanks for your time." I made a note of Roger Dayton's address, just in case I needed to talk with him.

My next stop was the *Herald* building. I walked, even though it was going to be almost as far back to the Jeep as it would have been to go home. I might as well have left the car in the driveway after all.

The security guard remembered me, and so did Roseanne Urrutia.

"Christmas 1977," I told her. "Both the *Examiner* and the *Herald*."

"They'll both say the same thing. They always did."

"I believe you. But I gotta check anyway, just in case."

She shrugged and directed me to the file case.

The man from the Recorder's Office was right—it was quite a story at the time. There was a lot on Farrell and his family, his wife and two sons, his brother, his father, who had owned both the Bunkhouse and the Old Corral before deeding them to his sons, and who also owned a bar in Las Vegas, the Branding Iron. Both brother and father—Cliff and Jared—denied knowing that Tommy was operating anything other than a bar and a cheap hotel for transients. If anybody other than the family got anything from whatever estate Farrell left, it didn't make the papers.

There was less on Rebecca Johnson, the hooker, just an interview with her stricken Mormon parents in Ely, who didn't understand how their little girl had gone wrong. And there were a few indignant quotes from civic leaders about the need to keep our city clean. I didn't see anything about a state bill to do something about prostitution for good and all, probably because there wasn't one.

There were no leads for the police to go on. Nobody had any reason to want Tommy Farrell dead. I found that puzzling—it seemed to me that any number of people might want to kill a guy who ran an illegal brothel, for any number of reasons, but what did I know. More important for me, there was no mention of Gary Hanrahan, no mention of Danny O'Neal, nothing that would tie the double murder to Danny's disappearance or Hanrahan's death.

I wasn't sure what I had expected to find, but I was disappointed anyway. Nothing seemed to go anywhere. I thanked Roseanne Urrutia for her help and left. I thought about asking the security guard to see if Sandra was around, but I really didn't feel like company.

On my way back to the Jeep, I detoured to Wingfield Park. I wandered out onto the island, walked to the tip, where I could watch the Truckee's silvery rills—which there in town were sort of brown and sluggish—flowing on either side, and sat down on the dry grass. I had to decide which long shot to bet on next—the Farrell murder, the Hanrahan murder, or the Vegas hooker. None of them looked like winners that would lead me to Danny. The Farrell murder was fifteen years old, the cops wouldn't want me nosing around the Hanrahan murder, and finding a particular hooker in Vegas would be worse than looking for the proverbial needle in the haystack. That's doable, if you want the needle badly enough—all you have to do is burn down the haystack, and what doesn't burn is your needle. Sift the ashes and you've got it. No harder than cutting the Gordian Knot.

The river was low, but it still made a satisfying splash when it went over the weir. I tried to remember which Greek philosopher commented that you never step into the same river twice. That was closer to what I was trying to do—step into a fifteen-year-old river, expecting to find the same drops of water. Or find one drop of water, when I knew where it was two years ago. The possibilities were endless, dumb, and this wasn't getting me anywhere.

I left the park and went back to my Jeep. I wasn't ready to go home, so that meant a little more time on the Farrell murder. At least I had an address to go to—the one I had copied down for Roger Dayton, which turned out to be a townhouse near Virginia Lake. My first reaction was that it was a little upscale, a little classy, for somebody who would own the Bunkhouse. My second reaction was that the Bunkhouse was probably fairly profitable, and I wasn't looking at Buckingham Palace.

My third reaction was surprise. I pushed the button for the doorbell, waited, pushed it again, started to get annoyed at the delay, and then heard a deadbolt turn. The man who opened the door, still in his bathrobe shortly before noon, was the bouncer from the Bunkhouse.

"You're Roger Dayton," I said. "You own it."

"You got me," he said, smiling, showing his two gold-capped teeth. "But I still don't remember your father. Ev told me," he added, when I started to ask how he knew.

"Yeah, okay. How about Tommy Farrell?"

"Can't say I knew him, either."

"But you must have known about him. Can you tell me anything about his murder? Anything that wasn't in the papers? I looked up the story."

"Probably not much. But come on in, if you like. I was just making some coffee, and you're welcome to join me."

"Thanks."

Dayton stepped back, and I walked into a narrow entry, with steps to my right leading down into a living room, and a long flight of stairs to my left. He gestured toward a grouping of three small green sofas and a coffee table that was arranged facing a fireplace. A log was glowing, radiating just enough heat to make the room comfortable. There was an oak entertainment center in the far corner of the room, but the furniture arrangement wasn't conducive to watching television. I didn't see a lot of personal stuff around.

"Take anything in your coffee?"

I shook my head. I sat in one of the sofas. I liked it—it was chosen with tall people in mind. Dayton returned with two mugs in his hand, gave me one, and sat on the sofa across from me.

"So why're you interested in the Farrell murder?" he asked.

"I'm looking for a reason Danny O'Neal might have had to leave town, something he might have been running from. An unsolved murder of somebody he used to work for has possibilities."

Dayton raised his eyebrows. "You think your daddy killed Farrell?"

"I hope not—I sure don't know any motive he might have had. But I need to find out more." I tasted the coffee. It was strong enough to make my scalp tingle.

"Motive was the problem the police had, as I remember. Couldn't figure out why anybody would want to kill Tommy Farrell."

"That's nuts. How about his wife? How about the girl's parents? A Mormon hit man—an Avenging Angel who decided to take the girl out, too, as long as he was there."

"A Morman hit man, that's good." He chuckled. "When I bought the place, so much time had gone by that most of the talk had died down, and it had been closed so long that none of the same girls came back. But that don't mean the story never came up. The wife was supposed to be one of those long-suffering souls who thought her trials on earth would help her out in heaven. Not the kind who'd pick up a shotgun and start blasting. And I never heard anything about the girl's parents. Or the girl. Farrell tried them all out before he hired them, and then once a month or so after that, just to make sure he'd have satisfied customers. Don't know that there was anything special about this one."

"Did you hire new girls?"

He chuckled again. "You wearing a wire or something? The place makes money. I don't need to commit felonies. I also don't expect people checking into those rooms to have five pieces of matched luggage."

"And it doesn't surprise you when they pay in cash."

"That's right. The names on the credit cards and the names on the register probably don't match, and I don't ask."

"Who inherited the property from Farrell? Who'd you buy it from?"

"The wife got it. Not too surprising when she didn't want it."

"The newspaper said that Farrell got the property from his father. The old man didn't want it back?"

"I don't know. Never heard. He's supposed to be a tough old buzzard. Now there's somebody who'd pick up a shotgun and start blasting." He laughed as he said it, to show I wasn't supposed to take it as a real suggestion that Farrell Senior had blown away his son.

"Do you know him well?"

"Only by reputation. I've heard he lives out in the mountains somewhere. He was an old guy then—probably about a hundred and ten by now."

"On the subject of old guys—did you know Gary Hanrahan?"

"Only by sight." He put his coffee mug on the table and shook his head sadly. "I didn't know his name. Ev pointed out the article in the paper to me, the one that said Hanrahan'd been shot. Reminded me who he was. He'd been around a lot when I first bought the place, not so much in the last few years."

"Losing interest in the girls?"

"No—because he didn't have much to start. I don't remember ever seeing him leave with one. That wasn't what brought him in."

Dayton said it so seriously that I felt bad, as if I'd taken a cheap shot at a dead man.

"Then what did bring him in?"

"I don't rightly know. I think it may have just been habit, he kept coming in because he had for so long. He wasn't in so much after I raised the drink price and the cover charge."

"Did he hang out with Watson a lot?"

"I don't know what Ev does with his days, but not at night, no. They'd nod to each other, maybe, but Ev treated him just like anybody else who'd buy him an occasional drink."

"Do you have many guys who just come in for a drink?"

"Can't say I do. There were probably a few before I raised prices, but I can't say I miss them."

I took a final sip of coffee, felt my scalp tingle again, and set the mug down.

"Want a refill?" he asked.

"No thanks. But I like your coffee. It's the kind of coffee that makes you understand how coffee becomes an addiction."

"Yeah, it is that. This is espresso grind coffee, just brewed in a regular drip pot, and if I'm away from it for a day, I start getting these bad headaches."

"Thanks for warning me." I stood and held out my hand. "And thanks again for intervening the other night."

"No problem."

He walked me to the door. The townhouse had felt too warm after just a few minutes, and I was glad to be outside again. If I hadn't just spent all that time brooding at the Truckee, I would have walked over to Virginia Lake, and brooded there for a while, this time on the apparent contradiction that Dayton could have strippers and— maybe—hookers in his employ, and own that truly sleazy establishment, without being a totally offensive human being.

I brooded in the Jeep, on the way home, still wondering if there were any connections here, wondering if I shouldn't go to Vegas just because that was the last place Danny had been seen by somebody I had actually talked to, wondering if that would just be a vain activity to encourage the illusion of progress. I considered calling Ely, to see if the dead hooker's parents were still there, but just thinking about asking them questions about a daughter who had been murdered years earlier made me feel sick. The Mormon hit man seemed like a really bad joke once I thought about it.

There were no messages on my answering machine and nothing in the mail that helped. But the balance of my musing shifted when I turned on the computer. Rudy's ex-girlfriend in the bartender's union had come through. Danny O'Neal had worked in Vegas just a couple of years ago. At a bar called the Branding Iron.

Chapter

8

THANKS TO WARREN Beatty, every student of popular culture believes that the modern city of Las Vegas was founded by gangsters. Official Nevada histories are far more circumspect, preferring to emphasize that The Meadows was a common stopping place on the Old Spanish Trail from Santa Fe to Los Angeles, also the site of a Mormon mission, and that the boom actually started in 1931 with the influx of workers for the construction of Hoover Dam. An unnamed hotel proprietor from Los Angeles who was stranded in the desert, waiting uncomfortably in the heat while his companion walked for help, and who vowed to build a luxury hotel on the spot later known as the Strip, is mentioned only in passing and only in some histories.

Flying into Las Vegas, I have always found it easier to accept the Bugsy Siegel story than the one describing Indians growing pumpkins, corn, and melons along the banks of the Colorado River. Las Vegas looks as artificial as Lake Mead, with its arbitrary shoreline. There's desert, which from the air looks brown and lifeless, and then all of a sudden there's a city, with no obvious reason for existing—no port or harbor, no farming community, no manufacturing or industry to speak of, no natural wonders like the Grand Canyon or Niagara Falls.

While it might have been more practical to drive to Las Vegas, rather than charter the Cherokee and then rent a car, the truth is that I wanted to fly, and Mom generously agreed to foot the bill. She had paid for the flying lessons, or Al had, so that I could get a private pilot's license, and she must have suspected at the time that she would end up paying for me to use it.

Besides, flying would save me a lot of wear and tear. I could fly down in the afternoon, stop by the Branding Iron in the early evening, spend one night in a cheap hotel, talk to Sam in the morning to let him know I was hanging in and to find out if he had thought of anything helpful, and fly back. Twenty-four hours, there and back. Four hours in a plane, instead of fourteen in a car.

I radioed Clearance Control for the small charter terminal next to McCarran International and got permission to land, then taxied around to the private-plane parking lot where I could tie the Cherokee down. I walked past the office and over to the main terminal where I could rent a car. An enthusiastic young woman helped me to a tiny, tinny Toyota. That's one of the things I hate about renting cars. You have to pay extra to get a Ford that isn't any better than a Toyota. I always buy American, even though I realize I can't always be certain that the car, or whatever, was actually assembled by American workers from American-made parts, but sometimes I compromise my principles and rent foreign. The irony, of course, is that the Toyota was probably made in America anyway, to get around the "voluntary" import limits.

I took Rancho Drive down to Bonanza Road and turned left, toward downtown, looking for the street the Branding Iron was on. This was the flat, ugly part of Las Vegas, not to be confused with the built-up, ugly part. There may be an attractive section of town, but I've never seen it. I have a

natural bias in favor of mountains, and while the southern
tip of the Sierras is close enough that on clear days it looks
only a mile or two away, Las Vegas itself just sort of squats
like a toad in the sand. Some of the downtown buildings are
a chintzy attempt to re-create a sense of the Old West, but
mostly it looks like New Money and Old Heartache. I had
landed fairly late, and the sunset over the far mountains was
pretty enough, but I had to drive away from it.

The bar was just the other side of the Las Vegas
Expressway, between a souvenir store offering live cactus
and Indian pottery on one side and Harry's Racing and
Sports Book on the other. And it was a real downer, walking
in the door and realizing that my father had worked there
only a couple of years before. Almost, but not quite, as bad
as walking into the Bunkhouse. I could try to kid myself that
the Bunkhouse might have looked better fifteen years ago.
The Branding Iron was encrusted with more than two years
of dirt. And it probably hadn't looked better when it was
new.

A neon sign in the window had promised both beer and
billiards, and most of the room was taken up by three pool
tables. Two were unused, the low conic lamps unlit, the
balls quiet in their racks. At the third, one old man was
slowly, casually clearing the table. He was bent over, under
the light, and I could only see his weathered hands. The
right one was missing the last two fingers.

Four people were sitting at the bar, none interacting. The
bartender, who was watching me from a face that had been
hit so many times it rippled from nose to ears, was a round,
balding man in his forties. His beefy forearms stretched out
of rolled-up sleeves as he leaned against the bar. I tried
imagining Danny in his place. I couldn't do it.

"What can I do for you?" he asked as I slid onto a stool
several feet removed from the next nearest patron.

"I'm looking for a man who used to work here. Danny O'Neal."

He shook his head. "Never heard of him."

"Then how do I find Jared Farrell?"

"Can't help you."

"Come on. You're not going to say you never heard of him. He owns this place."

"And he comes in now and then, not often. But I can't help you get in touch with him."

"Why not?"

"Orders. Mr. Farrell likes his privacy."

I pulled out a card and placed it on the bar. He didn't react. Behind me, I heard the crack of cue hitting ball.

"Please give him my card and ask him to call me if he's willing to talk with me."

"Sure. Glad to." He didn't even glance at the card.

I left feeling even more depressed than when I went in. I negotiated a route through the one-way streets of downtown Las Vegas, watching neon give way to cement-block apartment buildings, tract homes, and minimalls as I headed south toward the Strip. I found a small motel that advertised one person, one night, for $19.95, and turned into the parking lot. The young man in the office was protected by the kind of plastic shield that isolates cashiers in all-night gas stations. I pushed a credit card through the slot at the bottom, explaining I was by myself, and it was just for the night. He held the card until he could compare my signatures, then gave me a key and directions to my room.

I probably would have been smarter to go to one of the Strip hotels, where I could have gotten a better room for a bit more, and Mom was paying anyway, but I couldn't deal with the crowds just then. I wanted quiet. So there I was, alone except for a cockroach that tried to hide under the sink when I turned the bathroom light on. I grabbed a wad of toilet paper, picked him up, and flushed him down.

The room smelled of stale cigarette smoke and dried-out dreams. It was cold, and the only sources of light were two bedside lamps with forty-watt bulbs. The dim glow made it colder. I turned on a tall gas heater embedded in the wall next to a tiny closet, but I didn't hear the hoped-for whoosh when the gas came on, just a soft hiss. If I was lucky, this heater could take the chill out of the room by dawn. I left my flight bag on the heavy, rough indigo bedspread and went out to find a coffee shop. One without Keno. Even though playing is habit, I do it because I always believe that one of these days I'm going to win big. That night I knew I'd just lose. I didn't feel anything good was going to happen to me in Las Vegas.

After a hamburger and a beer at a coffee shop, I returned to the motel. I thought about calling Sam while I was out—the room didn't have a phone—but I was afraid he would ask me over, insist I stay with them, and I just didn't want to do that. I lay down on the scratchy bedspread and stared at the blank television set mounted near the ceiling, like one in a hospital. Harder to steal that way. I didn't turn it on.

Nothing was coming easily. The whole case—my father, the case—felt like one damn dead end after another. Literally. Gary Hanrahan, Tommy Farrell. And poor Rebecca Johnson. And two blind corners. Jackie Ellis and Jared Farrell. I was uncomfortably aware that I had made no effort to check the records at the Nevada State Prison to see if one Danny O'Neal had been a guest anytime during the eighties. I argued myself out of that one because if he had been in jail, he could have been anywhere from Folsom to Attica. I knew, too, that I was simply having trouble coming up with a plan to find him.

For years after Danny left, I kept expecting to see him again. I thought he'd be waiting for me one day after school. The summer I worked as a cashier at the Crest Theater, I watched faces, faces on the street, faces in the line. Everybody I knew came to the Crest Theater that summer, sooner or later. Everybody but Danny.

And the mail. Especially around my birthday, but sometimes around Christmas, too, I'd start hoping. Even when he still lived with us, Danny had been pretty erratic about remembering my birthday. Some years it had been a big celebration, going out for dinner and a movie, some years it just slipped by with one present that was obviously Mom's choice. He didn't even pretend he knew what it was before I opened it. After he left, I didn't get so much as a card from him. As if he erased me from his life, or wanted to be erased from mine.

Once I turned twenty-one, I'd check the face of the bartender every time I walked into a club, the face of the mechanic every time I had my car serviced. I knew he had left Reno—but he didn't seem like someone who would stay away. Reno was his home, and even if you can't go home again, some people keep trying. Danny would have been one of them, I had been certain.

As years went by, I became less certain. I wasn't sure when I had stopped checking faces, stopped hoping for a birthday note, but it had been a while. It had been long enough that it was painful to start again, a pain that had been made worse by Sam's story and the realization that the face I was likely to find—if I found him—wasn't the one I wanted, wasn't the one I had longed for during a lonely, alienated adolescence.

Shit.

The sheets were cold and rough and the mattress was lumpy. The heater pinged every time I was almost asleep, and my muscles jerked in response. I got up at first light, threw some cold water on my face, left the room key on the small vanity, beneath the cloudy mirror, and went out to find coffee and a telephone.

Coffee came first, at the same corner restaurant where I had eaten the night before. I drank two cups before I decided the household would be up.

Moira answered the phone.

"Come on over," she said when I told her I was in Las Vegas. "Doc's already left for his eight o'clock class, and Sam isn't up yet, but I have a fresh pot of coffee on, and you're welcome to share it with me."

She gave me directions to a house just the other side of UNLV, in a middle-class neighborhood of one-story frame houses that looked a couple of decades older than the campus. I haven't seen the whole campus, but what I have seen is ugly and raw-looking. Flat, like the city. With exposed beams of half-finished dorms attesting to its rapid growth. So somebody must like it, even if I don't.

I spotted the Winnebago before I saw the address, and pulled over to park in front of a faded yellow frame house that would have been indistinguishable from its neighbors except for the two Harleys that shared the driveway with the large motor home. The yard was brown and untended. Moira opened the front door when I was halfway up the walk.

"Sam's still asleep," she explained. "I wanted to beat the doorbell."

I followed her into a living room that was warmer and more homelike than I had expected. A sofa and two wingbacked chairs were covered in muted autumn colors, orange and brown, with ruffles around the bottom. A tortoiseshell cat gazed at me through green eyes from one of the chairs, daring me to disturb her. I sat on the sofa. The coffee table in front of me had papers spread out on it, as if someone used it for a desk. A cut-rate pine entertainment center was the focal point of the room, overloaded with TV set, stereo components, books, and a plastic plant. An area on the other side of the front door held a dining table with curved legs that had also been commandeered for a desk.

Moira excused herself and returned almost immediately with two unmatched pottery coffee mugs. She had remembered that I didn't take anything in mine. I watched her sit in the unoccupied chair, cross her legs, sip her coffee. There was something about her that reminded me of my mother, even though Mom was not likely to hang out in faded jeans and dingy sweatshirt, and Mom would have washed the traces of gray right out of her hair. Mom always wore makeup, too, even to go to the grocery store, and Moira's face was scrubbed, her eyebrows unplucked. But Moira was slim and tightly self-possessed and clear-eyed and ageless in the same way Mom was.

The cat arched her back, stretched, and hopped gracefully from her chair to Moira's lap.

"You must have a lead on Danny," she said, stroking the cat. "Something to bring you to Las Vegas."

"Not a lot. I heard he'd been working at a bar called the Branding Iron, but nobody there remembered him. I thought as long as I was in town, I'd drop by to see if either you or Sam had remembered something that might help."

"Actually, I did remember something. The name of the studio where Jackie Ellis said she was taking dancing lessons."

"Why the hell didn't you call me?" It came out too loud, too abrasive, but I was stunned.

She didn't seem offended. "You could have changed your mind, decided not to look for Danny after all. I didn't want to encourage you, if you decided to give it up. And I thought you'd show up here sooner or later if you were still on his trail."

"Yeah, well, I'm here."

"I didn't check to see if the studio is still in business."

"That's okay. I will." I put down my coffee mug and stood, ready to leave.

"Freddie, it's too early. The studio won't be open. And Sam would be hurt if you left without saying hello."

I didn't believe Sam would be hurt, but I did believe the studio wouldn't be open. I sat back down.

"What was the name of the studio?"

"Rene Dupree. I remembered because it sounded like a name you'd give a Frenchman in a joke."

"Anything else you remembered?"

"No. And please lighten up, just a little. I'm not your enemy."

I was thinking about that, not certain of my response, when I was stopped by a voice from the archway that led to the rest of the house.

"Freddie. Hell. I was about to say, why didn't you wake me up, but I guess you did."

Sam was standing there, gray hair uncombed, in a purple terry-cloth bathrobe, loosely sashed. I caught a glimpse of gray chest hair and naked shins before I looked back at my coffee.

"Get a cup, join us," Moira said. "And get dressed."

"Be back in a minute."

Silence. Moira was waiting for me to say something.

"What's your cat's name?" I asked.

"Lucky Lucy."

"She has pretty eyes."

Moira nodded, accepting the peace offering. I could hear water running, old pipes rattling. I wished Sam would hurry.

"Where are you staying while you're here?" Moira asked.

"I just got in yesterday, and I planned on flying back today." Even as I said it, I knew that if anything came of my trip to the dance studio, I would have to stay over at least one more night.

"But now you won't leave, because you'll try to track down Jackie Ellis. You're welcome to stay here—the couch pulls out into a reasonably comfortable bed."

I was working on a polite refusal when Sam rumbled, again in the archway, "Of course you'll stay here."

He had donned a black turtleneck and jeans, and his hair looked as if he had run wet fingers through it. He had brought the coffeepot with him, and he refilled both my cup and Moira's. I should have refused—I was getting wired—but I thanked him. He started to set the pot on the papers on the coffee table. Moira saved what appeared to be some student quizzes by shoving a magazine under the pot, disturbing Lucky Lucy, who had to resettle herself.

"So what have you found out?" he asked.

"I found out Danny was working just a couple of years ago at a bar called the Branding Iron. Do you know it?"

"Can't say I do. But I don't spend a lot of time in bars."

"Did Danny ever mention a guy named Gary Hanrahan? Or Tommy Farrell?"

"I don't remember Hanrahan. Farrell sounds familiar, but it's a common name. Do they remember him?"

"Well, Farrell's been dead for about sixteen years, but his brother Cliff remembers Danny. Won't tell me anything. And Hanrahan remembered Danny, but now he's dead."

"How?"

"Somebody shot him."

"You think Danny's connected with the deaths?"

"I don't want to. But Farrell's murder is something he could have been running away from. The time was right."

Sam shook his head. "Danny wasn't a murderer."

"He killed people in the war, you said he did." That was the wrong thing to say, I could tell from Sam's face. "I know, you're going to tell me that was different."

"It was."

"But you can't say he wasn't capable of murder."

"No, I guess I can't. I can't even say that about you. You look like you can take care of yourself, and under the right circumstances, that might include murder." He examined me as he said it. When I didn't react, he continued. "It sure don't feel right, though. Why would he have done it?"

"I don't know. Unless it was money—unless he was paid."

"You that willing to think ill of him?"

"No, goddamn it, no, I'm not." Sam got to me again. Something about him just burrowed in. "I just can't think of any good reasons why he started running and disappeared and showed up and had money. But I keep slipping on the bad reasons as if they were banana peels." I put my coffee cup down and stood up again. "Staying here probably isn't a good idea."

"Sure it is. Relax." I sat down, but I didn't exactly relax. Sam went on, "The trouble is where all that leads you. Danny kills Farrell for money, runs away for years, messing himself up, and then shows up back in Reno just in time to kill Hanrahan so he won't blab. I don't buy it, and if you did, you'd be in Reno looking for him, not chasing a cold scent in Las Vegas."

"Maybe."

"Definitely," Moira said. "You're in Las Vegas because you want another explanation, one where Danny isn't a murderer. And for what it's worth, I agree with Sam on that, too. Killer-for-hire doesn't sound like Danny."

I felt better, hearing that. Killer-for-hire had been swimming around in the undertow of my mind, and I hadn't wanted to let it surface. I wondered again how well Moira had known Danny. This time I didn't ask her.

"This is a heavy conversation for a man with an empty stomach." Sam broke what could have turned into a long silence. "Anybody but me want breakfast?"

"I ate earlier, with Doc," Moira said.

"Freddie?"

"Sure, I could eat something."

I followed him out to the kitchen. I wasn't particularly hungry, but I didn't want to be left with Moira, and I had a prurient interest in the rest of the house—how many bedrooms and how they were divided. I glanced down the hall to the right as we turned left. Although I couldn't be sure, it seemed to me that there were only three doors in the other direction, and one led to a bathroom.

The kitchen looked as if everybody cooked, and nobody was assigned to clean up. The counters—white tile with blue trim—were stacked with dirty dishes and open cereal boxes. The cabinet doors were thick with old paint and new fingerprints. In one corner was a small wooden table with four chairs, two unusable unless the table was pulled away from the wall and into the center of the room.

I sat at one of the usable chairs and watched Sam fry up some bacon and eggs. I was beginning to feel comfortable with him, if not with Moira. It felt okay that I didn't want to talk anymore.

When we had finished eating, he cleared the table and started working on the rest of the kitchen as well. He turned down my offer of help.

"Why don't you just go on and check out that dance studio," he said. "I'll pretty much be here today, so you can come on back when you feel like it."

"Thanks. I will. Is there a telephone directory, so I can look up the address?"

"In the living room, under the coffee table."

Moira had disappeared from the living room, and Lucky Lucy was asleep on the chair. The address was on Flamingo Road, not far away. I let Sam know I was leaving. I didn't look for Moira.

Rene Dupree Dance Studio was on the second floor of a minimall a few blocks east of the Strip, over a donut shop and a laundromat. A sign on the door offered ballet, jazz, and modern dance. Next to it was a black-and-white publicity photo of a slender, muscular man with a chiseled face wearing a leotard and tights. It was one of those posed, arty photos with stark contrasts, not much gray. Even so, I could tell his hair was gray. That was the only sign of age.

I walked into a small reception area, just big enough for a desk, which was unoccupied at the moment. The walls were decorated with more arty shots of the same man, some of them with other dancers as well, and a few autographed pictures of the kind of celebrities who headline the showrooms in Las Vegas. Wayne Newton. Debbie Reynolds. A sign listed the schedule for September and October, by time, type of class, and teacher. Besides Dupree, there were four other names listed as teachers. The sign also advertised a fall special—$150 in advance for unlimited classes.

An open door to the left led to a large room with hardwood floors, mirrored walls, and a bar. Two women were stretching at the bar, a third on the floor. The one on the floor was wearing chartreuse leg warmers. A closed door behind the desk was unmarked. I wasn't certain whether it was an inner office, a changing area, or a bathroom. I decided not to check.

"Is Rene Dupree around?"

I stood in the doorway to the studio and addressed the question to all three women, since none of them looked at me.

The woman on the floor glanced up, hands on the ankles of her Day-Glo warmers, back almost flat. She had to be double-jointed to hold a position like that.

"He's here," she said. "He'll be back in a minute to start the class."

Her face was back on the floor before I could thank her.

Two more thin young women in tights topped with short, torn T-shirts, blond hair in ponytails, sweatbands around foreheads, scampered out of a door toward the rear of the studio and joined the pair at the bar. Another followed, plopping to the floor next to the chartreuse leg warmers. The six were a motley, barefoot crew, stripes and solids, faded and fresh, and I wondered what Degas would have done with them. No tutus here.

A force brushed past me, materializing into Rene Dupree, in black tank top and tights, older and wirier in the skin than in the photograph.

"I'd like to talk—" I began.

"Not now!" he snapped. "You'll have to wait until after the class." He strode to the mirror, whirled, and faced the group, not pausing to see whether I would wait or not. "On the floor!"

The six women, and one more who rushed through the door as he spoke, dropped into a ragged line in front of him, cross-legged.

"Breathe, two, three, four. And out, two, three, four. From the diaphragm, two, three, four. And out, two, three, four. Expand, two, three, four. And contract, two, three, four."

The women breathed in unison, as ordered.

I had to either leave, get coffee, and return, or stay and watch the class. I'd had enough coffee that morning.

And watching the class was kind of interesting. I couldn't tell whether the class was jazz or modern, because I'm not certain what the difference is, but whatever it was, the group knew what it was doing. After about twenty minutes of warm-up exercises on the floor, they spent the rest of the time working on a complicated routine to music from *West Side Story*. The women were good, even without tutus.

When he had run them through their paces for the last time, four bounded toward the rear door, and three clustered around him for some kind of conference. Only after they were satisfied did he look over and nod to me. I waited while he crossed the studio.

"Beginning classes are at six o'clock," he said. "Ballet on Monday and Wednesday, jazz Tuesday and Thursday, modern on Friday. Twenty dollars per class, but we offer reduced rates if you pay a month in advance."

"I'm not a dancer," I told him.

"I know that. You're starting too late to ever become a professional, but taking classes is still a good choice. You're tall and long-limbed, and dance classes will teach you to work from your center, to control your body and the space around it."

It wasn't a putdown, it was simply an assessment. What surprised me was that I hadn't realized he'd looked at me long enough to make it.

"I don't plan on taking classes. In truth, I'm looking for a student of yours, Jackie Ellis. At least she used to be your student."

He appraised me through narrow, dark eyes in a pale, lined face.

"You ought to take classes. Dancing would get rid of those hunched shoulders. And I don't give out information on students, present or former. That's a firm policy."

I unhunched my shoulders and controlled the space around me by barring the doorway with one of my long limbs as he started to walk past me.

"I'm not a bill collector, and she isn't in trouble. I need to talk with her because she's the only link I have to my father."

"I'm sorry," he said, without any attempt at sincerity. "It's still a firm policy. I don't give out information on students."

"Okay. But if you have a current phone number for her, could you call her? Could you give her a message that I need to talk with her? A phone number where she could call me?"

"Absolutely not." He slipped smoothly underneath my arm. "I hope you change your mind about the dance lessons, though."

He walked through the door behind the desk without looking back.

I thought about following him, I thought about waiting for him to come out, but it didn't seem useful unless I could come up with a new approach.

The dancer with the chartreuse leg warmers, now wearing jeans and a Stardust sweatshirt, caught up with me as I was walking down the stairs. Her brown hair hung loose around a thin face still flushed from the class.

"I overheard you asking about Jackie Ellis," she said. "Why are you looking for her?"

"I'm really looking for a guy named Danny O'Neal—my father. I think she may be able to help me."

"Then she's not in trouble?"

"Not that I know of."

"Oh. Too bad. I was hoping."

"Why?"

We paused in the parking lot. She shifted her gym bag, tan canvas with a Warner Bros. logo, over her shoulder.

"We used to be roommates, and when she moved out, she stiffed me on two weeks rent and a month's utilities, including a fat phone bill."

"Do you know where she is now?"

"I wish I did."

"How long ago did she leave?"

"About a month ago."

Only a month. My heart started beating. I don't know when it had stopped, but at that moment it started.

"Have you tried to find her?"

The woman shrugged. "There didn't seem much point. If she had wanted to pay me, she would have. What am I going to do, beat her up?"

"No, I guess not." If Jackie Ellis needed money, getting information from her would be easy. Once I found her. "Tell you what—if you check off which calls are Jackie's, I'll pay for the phone bill." Or Mom would.

"Deal," the woman said. "And I'll tell you everything I know about her if you'll pay the electric bill, too."

I held out my hand, and she took it.

"I only live a few blocks away, so I walked," she continued. "If you want to talk now, we have to take your car."

I pointed to the Jeep. She threw her bag in the back and settled into the passenger's seat.

She directed me back toward the university, then west, then told me to park in front of a squat, two-story apartment building, concrete sprayed industrial rose, that stretched along a driveway perpendicular to the street. On the way, we introduced ourselves. The name she gave me was Starla Scott, and I didn't push it.

We walked past an entryway of gravel studded with plastic flowers and up a concrete stairway. The apartment was on the second floor, about halfway back.

"Would you like a glass of water?" Starla asked as she opened the door. "I don't really have anything else to offer you. I don't cook, and I don't eat here."

"Nothing. That's okay." I sympathized.

The narrow living room was dotted with throwaway furniture—two blue canvas chairs, the kind with weird aluminum frames that used to look modern, a tan beanbag, and a white table that looked as if it had been picked up at a garage sale.

"I'll get the phone bill," she said.

I sat in one of the low-slung canvas chairs. My knees came almost up to my chin. There was nothing to look at, so I closed my eyes and waited for Starla. I could hear her checking an answering machine, a male voice, but not what the message was. I opened my eyes again when I heard her returning.

"Here," she said, handing me the phone bill. "I already checked off her calls, when I was figuring out what she owed me. You can have it for fifty-nine ninety-eight. And it's another thirty-eight fifty for the electric bill. Jackie had a habit of leaving the air conditioner on high, even when she went out."

I had to stand up, not an easy task, to get my wallet out of my jeans. I took out five twenties and handed them to her. This time I sat in the beanbag, which wasn't much of an improvement. Starla took one of the canvas chairs. She was graceful and long-legged, and somehow she looked right in it.

"How did you and Jackie Ellis become roommates?" I asked.

"I met her at Rene's. I don't go every morning, and neither did she, but we were sometimes in the same classes. A couple of times we had lunch afterward, first because we both headed for the yogurt shop, and then because we liked each other. About six months ago, she told me she needed a place to stay. I said I had room and could use help with expenses. She moved in, and then she moved out."

"And you didn't try to find her?"

Starla shook her head. "She didn't show up for dance classes anymore, so I didn't think it would do any good. Jackie loved the classes, and if she'd had any money, she would have been there."

"What did she do to make money when she had it?"

"Well—various things." Starla paused, looking at me expectantly, as if she hoped I might rescue her. I didn't. "Jackie had an agent, and sometimes she got modeling jobs, or worked as an extra when there was a movie shooting here. She auditioned whenever there was a new show at one of the clubs, but there aren't really that many chorus jobs available."

This time the pause was so long that I prompted her.

"What else?"

"Sometimes she got money from men."

"Turning tricks?"

"Yeah, I guess so. I never asked for details."

"If she was hooking—even occasionally—" I added because of the expression on Starla's face, "I don't understand why she was broke. Unless she was sick or got busted."

"She didn't get busted, and I don't think she was sick. I think she got scared."

"Of what?"

"I don't know." She leapt from the chair with the grace of a startled fawn and took two steps to the unadorned window that faced the cement walkway. There was nothing to see, and she turned back. "I think somebody threatened her, and I don't know who or why. I didn't ask."

"That's the other reason you didn't try to find her."

"Yeah, I guess."

"Was there anyone Jackie would have confided in?"

"I don't know. If she had any friends, I didn't meet them. She made a couple of long calls to the same number, you can see that on the bill, but I don't know whose number it was."

I looked at the telephone bill Starla had given me. Several of the red checks marked calls to a number in Bullfrog, Nevada. Wherever the hell Bullfrog was. And she was right, a couple of the calls were long ones.

"You think Jackie went to Bullfrog?" I asked.

"I think whatever happened to Jackie probably isn't funny," she answered.

"Then why did you say you hoped she was in trouble when you heard me asking about her?"

"Because I didn't know you, and I didn't want to say I thought she might need help. I wanted to find out about you first."

And get the money for the phone bill, no doubt.

She paced to the dining-room table, couldn't figure out what she was doing there, and paced back to the window.

"What happened that made you think she was scared or in trouble?"

Starla shrugged, her back to me. "Nothing, really. But it happens sometimes. Haven't you ever been in trouble?"

I ignored the question.

"Did she give you any clue that she was leaving?"

"No. She was just gone. I came back from a dance class, she had said she wanted to sleep in, and she was gone."

"Did you even try her agent? She must be keeping in touch with her agent."

"Maybe. You try her agent. Herb Utley. He's in the book."

"You don't like him."

"No." She said it flatly, in a way that ended the topic.

"Is there anything else you can give me that might help me find her? Did she leave anything here?"

"No. No, she took everything. There wasn't much, just her clothes."

"For a roommate, you don't know very much."

"Yeah, well, sometimes when you like people, you operate on trust."

Starla turned and looked at me when she said that, as if she really wanted me to understand, and I tried. I took out one of my business cards and wrote Sam's number on the back.

"I'll be in Vegas for another day or so, and then back in Reno. Call me if you think of anything that might help me find Jackie, will you?"

"Okay."

She didn't reach out to take the card, so I left it on the white plastic coffee table. I was at the door before she added, "I hope she's all right."

I drove slowly back to the household of three, wishing I had somewhere else to go. I was relieved that it was Sam who answered when I knocked.

"How'd it go?"

"Pretty well," I said, following him into the living room. "Is there a phone I can use? I'm going to run up some charges, but I'll pay you for them."

He pointed at a combination phone and answering machine almost hidden under the clutter on the dining-room table.

"Do what you need to do. I'll be in the back, if you want to talk."

I wasn't sure what "in the back" meant, but I didn't ask. I still couldn't decide how much I wanted to know about what was going on here. I nodded, and Sam nodded back, then left the room. Lucky Lucy hopped onto the table, scattering papers. She reminded me of Butch, and I had an impulse—quickly squelched—to go home and forget the whole thing.

I got Herb Utley's number from information and left a message on an answering machine. My next best chance was the number in Bullfrog, the one Jackie Ellis had run up a lot of charges talking to.

In Reno, I would have tried to find out whose number I was calling before picking up the phone. But I didn't have any connections in Vegas who might help except for Rudy Stapp, and it might take him too long. So I punched the digits for Bullfrog. I heard two rings at the other end.

"Farrell," a voice barked.

I had halfway expected an answering machine. I certainly hadn't expected "Farrell."

"Jared Farrell?" I asked.

A pause.

"Who's calling?"

"Freddie O'Neal. I'd like to talk with you."

Another pause.

"Forget it, kid. Go home and forget it."

The click and the silence told me he had hung up. I tried again, I let the phone ring fifteen times, but there was no answer. I hung up, counted to ten, and tried again. This time a busy signal. I put the phone down. Lucky Lucy and I stared at each other. I picked up the phone once more.

"This is Stapp Investigations," the machine answered.

"Rudy," I said after the beep. "Call me. Now. I need help."

I left Sam's phone number, hung up, and buried my face in my arms. Lucky Lucy purred in my ear.

Chapter 9

"WHEN THE ROAD gets rocky, you just gotta take a deep seat and a long rein and ride it out," Sam said as he walked into the dining room and found me slumped in a chair. "Nobody told you it was going to be a short trip. Or an easy one."

"Is that supposed to be comforting?"

"Just truthful. Want a cup of coffee?"

"No."

"How about a beer?"

That sounded better. "If I'm not drinking alone."

"Hell, I wouldn't let the child of an old buddy drink alone." He smiled, and I was glad he was there. "Why don't you move to a more comfortable chair while I'm getting them? You don't have to get stiff, just because you're miserable."

"Because I don't want to leave the phone. I'm expecting a couple of calls."

"Suit yourself."

The phone was still silent when he returned. He handed me a beer and took his own into the living room, where he lay down on the sofa and put his feet up.

"I guess you can sit in that straight chair until tomorrow," he said.

I didn't move. "Thanks for the beer."

"Was your day that bad?"

"Not really. I had a lead on Jackie Ellis—one that ties her to Jared Farrell."

"Jared Farrell?"

"I guess I didn't mention him. He's the owner of the Branding Iron, the last place I know of where Danny worked. Also the father of Cliff Farrell, who owns the Old Corral, and Tommy Farrell, who was murdered upstairs from the Bunkhouse, which he owned. Both in Reno, both places where Danny worked. Jackie made some long phone calls to a number in Bullfrog, wherever that is. Jared Farrell answered when I called."

"Bullfrog?" Sam choked on his beer.

Before I had a chance to ask why, the phone rang, and I pounced on it. The caller was Herb Utley, Jackie's agent. I had been intentionally vague when I left the message, so he might think I had a job for her. I explained that I was trying to locate a mutual friend and told him Jackie's former roommate thought he could help me get in touch with Jackie.

"Sorry, kid," he answered. "Jackie's out of town, has been for a month."

"Did she say where she was going?"

"No—just that she'd call when she got back."

"Could I give you my number? Would you let her know I want to talk with her?"

He sighed. "You can write a letter, and I'll hold it for her. I'd take your number, but I'd only lose it. Besides, she might want to know more about who this mutual friend is."

"The mutual friend is my father."

"Doesn't mean anything to me, and I don't know whether it would to her. Write a letter, best I can do."

"Shit," I said after I had hung up.

"You didn't really think her agent would help, did you?" Sam asked. "You're lucky he told you that much."

"Yeah, well, I have an honest voice."

"What next?"

"I have to wait for one more call, from a friend. Then I'm off to Bullfrog. And why did you choke?"

"Have you ever been to Bullfrog?"

"Never even heard of it."

"Bullfrog's near Beatty, it's a ghost town, one of the old mining centers. You'd be running up a lot of mileage on a rented car."

"You know it?"

"I've ridden most of the back roads in the state. Bullfrog." He shook his head. "I didn't think they had phone service there."

"Bullfrog is what it said on the bill, and somebody answered the phone."

Sam nodded. "Fine. We can return that rented car and leave first thing in the morning."

"We?"

"I don't have anything planned. Might as well take you on the bike. If you don't like riding tandem, Moira would probably let you borrow hers."

I had to think about that.

"How long would it take us to get there and back?"

"About two hours each way."

"I don't know, Sam. Thanks for the offer, but I think I'll just take the car."

"Scared?"

I bristled. "Of what?"

"I don't know. Seems to me a woman who flies her own plane wouldn't be scared of much. She might even learn to like having her own bike."

"I've never handled a bike. Would that slow us down?"

"Only on city streets, while you're getting used to it. Highway 95 won't have much traffic on a Wednesday morning, and we'll pick up speed in the desert."

"Why do you want to go?"

"Trusting soul, ain'tcha?" He grinned and sat up, to drain the last of the beer from the can. "I told you, I got nothing planned. On top of that, I'm getting interested in this search for Danny. And you're right—I don't like the idea of you going out in the desert by yourself to find this Jared Farrell, who may or may not be alone, and who might not want to talk to you."

I thought about bristling again, but he said it so amiably I couldn't. "I don't plan on doing anything dangerous. I'm just going to ask a few questions, and if he doesn't want to answer them, I'll come back."

"Fine. Then we'll have a pleasant day and a good ride, get to know each other a little."

"Okay. If Moira doesn't mind my borrowing her bike."

"She won't. But you can ask her when she gets back."

I wasn't looking forward to Moira's return, and I still couldn't figure out what it was about her that made me so uncomfortable. She and Doc came in together—preceded by the roar of the two Harleys pulling into the driveway and parking next to the Winnebago. And she thought it was just fine that Sam and I wanted to take a little trip to Bullfrog. She didn't even want to know why.

Doc opened beers for himself and Moira and turned on the television set. Geraldo was interviewing women who work as topless housemaids for a hundred dollars an hour. And they don't do windows.

I stayed in my corner of the dining-room table, pretty much ignored by the three of them, who seemed to have a clear, easy rhythm to their lives together. Doc watched TV, Sam and Moira commented, and all three drank beer. They looked up when the phone rang, but turned back when I said it was for me, the other call I had been waiting for.

"I can't tell you much," Rudy said. "Jared Farrell is a strange old guy who lives out in the desert somewhere. He's rumored to be a survivalist, and there may be some sort of paramilitary operation going on, so be careful if you're thinking about trying to find him."

Maybe having Sam with me wasn't such a bad idea.

"What kind of paramilitary operation?"

"I don't know. Farrell lost a couple of fingers from his right hand a few years ago. He said a shotgun went off while he was cleaning it, but I kept hearing rumors of something more. I didn't follow up on them because I didn't have a reason."

Shit. The old man shooting pool in the Branding Iron was missing two fingers from his right hand. I had him, but I didn't know it.

"Know anything about his son Tommy's death?"

"Nothing. Except it was a long time ago."

"Okay. Listen, maybe you could nose around a little. Just if you think of something that might help."

"Help what?"

"Help me figure out how my father is tied into this."

There was a pause at the other end.

"I'll get back to you," he said.

"We still on for tomorrow morning?" Sam asked after I hung up.

"Yeah. And thanks."

Letting the cats forage for one night was no problem, especially since I had left them plenty of dried food and water, but now it was going to be three, even if all went well. I was going to have to call Deke, ask him to look in on them. I decided to leave a message when I was certain he had left for work. I just didn't want the lecture.

After some discussion about what we should do for dinner, Moira ordered pizza. *Wheel of Fortune* turned into *Jeopardy*, which turned into a couple of Real Cop shows, but nobody seemed to care very much what they were watching. They might as well have been staring at the family hearth. During the late news, Moira brought out a sheet, a blanket, and a pillow, made Doc move off the sofa, and helped me make it into a bed. Out of habit, I kept one ear tuned for the weather, even though I wasn't flying in the morning. Clear and warm.

I listened to the ins and outs and slammed doors as Doc and Sam and Moira took turns with the bathroom, but I still wasn't certain who was sleeping where.

Doc was the first one out in the morning. I hadn't slept too well, partly because the sofa bed mattress was thin and lumpy, partly because I never sleep well without the cats, and partly because I'm not used to hearing toilets flush in the middle of the night. But I pretended to be asleep when Doc came through the living room. It was easier than trying to make polite early morning conversation with a man I didn't know.

By the time I heard Moira in the kitchen, I couldn't pretend to be asleep any longer. Too many toilets had flushed. Besides, she made pretty good coffee.

Moira didn't have much to say either. We were on our second cups of coffee and almost finished with the morning paper when Sam joined us.

"One cup of coffee," he said. "We'll stop for breakfast on the way. I'll follow you to the car rental, bring you back for the second bike, and then we'll head north."

"I've thought about that, and it doesn't make sense to turn the car in, when we're just going up and back in one day. And I may not have any reason to stay in Las Vegas after that, depending on what Farrell says. I might as well keep the car until tomorrow."

"Suit yourself." He drained his cup. "Then let's get started."

Getting started wasn't quite that simple, because Sam had to fill a couple of canteens with water for us to drink in the desert, make sure we both packed clothing in the saddlebags to cover any sudden changes in the weather—he ignored me when I said it was supposed to be clear—and find one of Doc's visored caps to shield my face from sun and wind.

"Those're good boots you're wearing," he said. "They'll protect your feet and ankles from the heat of the engine just fine."

All the preparations were beginning to annoy me, and I was wishing I had just taken off by myself in the car, when he was finally ready.

"Okay," Sam said when we were standing next to the bikes. "Ignition. Gas. Clutch. Gearshift. First, second, third, reverse." He pointed to each. "Watch me. Stay close, and raise your hand if you want to pull over. We'll take the first few blocks real slow."

He threw his leg over the bike easily, adjusted a pair of heavy dark glasses, turned the key, and slowly backed out of the driveway, waiting for me on the street. I almost yelled at him, wanting to know if that was really all he was going to say, all the instruction I was going to get in managing this machine, but I didn't. Moira's midnight-blue Harley looked like an alien being, bulging with a murderous strength, daring me to wrestle it into submission. I straddled the thing awkwardly, turned the key, and felt the engine kick in. I was surprised by the thrill of power that ran through the handlebars. Less than a plane, but there was a kick to it. I eased the bike into the street, mostly walking it backward, sensing its weight.

"Why don't you go around a block or two by yourself?" Sam said. "Be careful at corners, remember to lean into the turn. Come back when you're ready to go."

I started forward and stalled the bike, catching it with my feet. If it went over, it would be like having a horse fall on me. I glanced at Sam, but he wasn't watching. The next time I shifted into gear just fine, and the bike rolled smoothly down the street.

Two blocks and I turned. I felt the centrifugal force, even as slowly as I was going, and understood why he told me to lean in. By the time I got back to the house, I was shifting fairly smoothly and excited about taking it out on the highway.

Sam pulled around next to me. We turned right onto the Maryland Parkway, and I had a flash of vulnerability, riding the bike next to someone encased in steel. I was startled when Sam signaled for a left turn on Flamingo Road, but avoiding downtown made sense. Flamingo Road would take us straight to Highway 15, which we could take to 95 North.

I was so involved with learning to control the bike that I didn't even notice the flat and ugly part of Las Vegas or the two-block wide, adult theme park known as the Strip. As we took the on-ramp to 15, the Harley seemed to pick up speed of its own accord, again reminding me of a horse, one anxious to stretch its legs. At the edge of the city, just as 95 stopped being a freeway and started being a real highway, and just as I was starting to feel confident, Sam raised his hand and pointed to an exit. I followed him off the freeway and into the parking lot of a chain coffee shop.

"How're you doing?" he asked.

"Great. Just great."

"Fine. Then let's have breakfast."

I wasn't hungry and I wanted to keep going. But Sam ordered one of those big breakfasts with pancakes and bacon and eggs, so I ordered ham and eggs in case this was going to be it for the day.

"Don't drink too much coffee," he warned. "There are long stretches of highway with no place to relieve yourself but the other side of a rock."

I decided not to drink any.

After breakfast we had to fill the gas tanks. I was restless and annoyed. By myself, I would have been halfway to Beatty. Maybe all the way there, because I would have left before the second cup of coffee with Moira.

"You're lucky it's just the two of us," he said when I asked politely if we could proceed yet. "When you're on a big ride, with twenty or thirty bikes, it takes all day to get from here to Tonopah. Somebody always has to stop for something every few miles, and everybody else has to wait."

"Why? Why don't the rest of the bikes keep going?"

"Because then it wouldn't be a ride."

That didn't make sense to me, but I let it go.

We stuffed our jackets in the saddlebags, Sam tied a bandanna around his forehead, and we started our engines. I liked the feeling in the handlebars. Not as good as a plane's yoke, but not bad.

By the time we were back on Highway 95, it was almost noon and getting warm. My long-sleeved cotton shirt was just enough to shade me from the sun. Sam was down to a vest with ride buttons and a T-shirt that exposed the talons of the tattooed eagle. I was glad I had Doc's cap, because I could tell already that within a couple of hours the sun was going to feel not just warm, but hellishly hot. There's no shade between Las Vegas and Beatty except for a diner or two and a half-dozen bars in Indian Springs and Lathrop Wells.

The desert is a tricky place, a place of extremes. The

occasional road signs warning of flash floods seemed surreal in the white sun, but I'd been caught once near Vegas in a sudden cloudburst, when the rain came straight down all at once and the hard earth couldn't absorb it, and reality had twisted in my hands.

The trip would have been boring in a car. I would have paid attention to a few miles of desert, and then the straight, flat road would have become monotonous. I would have lost the sense of desolate majesty, quit looking at the chalky stria of the Yucca Mountains on one side and the dry, gray vegetation of the Amargosa Desert on the other, and turned on the radio and the air conditioner, spending the rest of the journey in comfortable isolation from my surroundings, wondering whatever possessed somebody to build a road through all that nothingness. I couldn't do that on the bike. I had to pay attention. It's that way in the Cherokee, too. You can't get bored when you know you're controlling a machine that can kill you if you slip.

Cars can do that, I know. But in a car, familiarity breeds not contempt, but at least a certain disrespect for power. Planes and bikes just wait for you to do that. Then they've got you.

I envied Moira the bike. Giving up the Jeep wouldn't be practical, but I wondered, as the sun beat down and my shirt was soaked with sweat and my mouth was dry with desert dust, if there wasn't some way I could afford a Harley as well. I had to watch Sam do it twice to figure out how to unscrew the cap and take a drink out of the canteen without pulling over and stopping the bike. Thirst and pride both came through, and I did it.

We stopped in Beatty at another gas station, on the junction of 95 and 374, marked by one blinking red light in the center of the intersection, to refill the tanks and drink a couple of Cokes. The water in the canteen had kept me from dehydrating, but I was ready for a caffeine-and-sugar fix. And my legs were stiff, the muscles tense, as if I'd been on a horse all morning. I needed to stretch.

Pop psychologists say that one of the differences between male friendships and female friendships is that women establish a bond through talking, and men through a shared activity. We couldn't talk on the highway—couldn't hear anything over the constant rumble of the engines. I wished I had thought to bring earplugs, because I couldn't hear for a few seconds even after the engines stopped. Still, I was amazed at how much Sam could communicate with a few simple gestures. And by the time we reached Beatty, I was starting to think of him as a friend. Maybe men have a point.

"Where do these towns come from?" I asked, looking around at the quiet gas station and convenience store, the almost deserted streets. Even in the shade, my shirt was sticking to me, and my boots seemed to be ankle deep in dust. I had finished half the Coke in one swallow, and my sense of adventure was restored. "How do they survive?"

"Well, Beatty survives because there's still some mining around, and some tourists who want to look at the ghost towns, but mostly because it's right at the entrance to Death Valley," Sam said. "In the spring, you can't get a motel room here, because of all the fellas from Detroit who want to test the new models in desert conditions. That's why the Sourdough Saloon serves pizza, and just down the street there's a grill with a salad bar and Mozart on the Muzak. I don't know about other towns."

I tried to imagine new cars in the dust. I finished my Coke and tossed the can into a receptacle.

"Let's get going."

"Bullfrog's only a couple of miles down the highway," he said. He had been leaning against the side of the small store, and he didn't move. "How do you plan to find Farrell?"

"It can't be very big. We'll ask when we get there."

"Okay." He seemed amused. "You want to eat something first?"

I thought of Mozart on the Muzak and shook my head. "All I wanted was the Coke."

"Then let's go."

We headed west into the Amargosa Desert on Highway 374, a road that would have taken us through Daylight Pass, between the Grapevine Mountains and the Funeral Mountains, and into Death Valley, but Sam slowed and gestured with his hand that we were turning right. The sign said "Rhyolite." I knew about Rhyolite—that was a ghost town on the maps, mostly because of the famous old house made of bottles.

The pavement was scarred, and I downshifted, feeling the Harley complain as it slowed, just in time for me to catch a much larger sign near what looked like some kind of ore-processing operation. That one said "Bullfrog."

Sam then pointed left, and I saw a small, hand-lettered sign with Bullfrog and an arrow on it. I swung onto the road, past a red barn with a large sign advertising antiques and a smaller sign saying "Closed," only to reach the end of the pavement. Another hand-lettered sign, complete with skull and crossbones, said "Go Back! Bullfrog is behind you!"

"Is this a joke?" I shouted at Sam over the roar of the two Harleys.

"If it is, I'm not the joker," he shouted back.

I turned off the engine and dismounted. My legs were still stiff, and I had to stand there looking around before I moved. I spotted two more hand-lettered signs. One, next to a partial stone wall that could have dated from the fall of Rome, said "Bullfrog Ice House, Built 1904." A rusted car of about the same vintage sat beside it. On the other side of the pavement, a sign in a pile of weeds said "Bullfrog bank was here."

"This is it?"

"This is it."

"What happened here?"

"I don't know. There was some sort of dispute over a mining claim, and everybody moved to Rhyolite. But that's pretty much gone, too. You can see what's left over there." He pointed to some ruins a mile or so away. "Where to now?"

I listened for the murmur of ghosts, hoping for a clue, but there wasn't even a breeze. There was sand, dead brush dried out from the heat, the antiques store, a mobile home beside it. Somebody—not a ghost—had dropped a partly eaten apple near the Bullfrog Ice House, and a beer can, too. And a dirt road marked "Private Drive" headed north into the rose-brown foothills, with telephone poles running alongside.

"That way," I answered. "Follow the telephone wires."

Sam looked up where the road curved around a pink sandstone bluff.

"You sure you want to do that? It says private."

I got back on the bike, started the engine, and turned onto the road. He was beside me a moment later.

We didn't get very far. Just around the curve, just before the packed earth road started back down into a desert valley, a gate blocked the path. It was one of those railroad-crossing arms, the kind that swings up when somebody in a guardhouse presses a button, and it stretched all the way across to a steep drop. The small guardhouse was in a narrow cleared area, flat against the side of the mountain. A pale young man in a work shirt and jeans was standing outside. He gestured for us to kill the engines.

"Sorry," he said. "You'll have to turn back. This is a private road, and you're trespassing."

"We're here to see Jared Farrell," I said. "He's expecting us."

"I don't think so. Mr. Farrell always tells me when he's expecting someone."

"Do you have a way of calling him?"

"Sure—there's a phone inside."

I nodded. "Then tell him Jackie Ellis is here."

He seemed puzzled, but didn't say anything before retreating to the guardhouse. I looked around, hoping there was a way past the gate. I didn't see one. And I couldn't see any other way to reach the floor of the shallow valley in front of us, or the cluster of buildings in the middle of it.

"Mr. Farrell says you're Freddie O'Neal," the young man called from the doorway. "But he says that as long as you're here, you can come on in. He'll meet you at the entrance to the house, that's the building right at the end of the road."

The arm swung up.

"Good for you," Sam muttered, clapping me on the shoulder.

We started the Harleys and drove through. The arm swung down behind us.

The descent was steep, and we stayed in low gear. About a mile of flat, open desert stretched like a sandy moat around the compound. We passed a couple of dark, barnlike buildings on our left, then found our way blocked by a large, two-story ranch house, with concrete steps leading up to a wide porch. There were other buildings beyond it, but this was clearly our destination. A closed garage with a parking area in front of it was on our right. We stopped next to a red Toyota pickup, the only vehicle in sight.

"Bad *feng shui*," Sam said.

"What?"

"Having a door right at the end of the road like that. The Chinese would say it brings back luck."

"Not for us, I hope."

"Not unless we moved in."

No way.

A man and a woman were standing in the doorway to the house, watching as we walked up the steps. The man was some indeterminate age past old and approaching ancient. He had a face as lined as tree bark, fringed with brush-cut white hair showing a dry brown scalp. He was wearing a khaki shirt and jeans, with a big sheriff's star set in the buckle. The woman next to him came barely to his shoulder and looked young enough to be his granddaughter. Her dancer's body was barely covered by tight white pants and a pink halter top, like a bikini bra. Ragged blond hair fell almost to her waist. She wasn't beautiful, but there was something striking about her face. I looked back at the man.

"Mr. Farrell, I presume."

He nodded.

"Hello, Sam," the woman said softly. "It's good to see you."

"Hello, Jackie," he answered.

I looked to Sam, suddenly afraid of betrayal. But he wasn't looking at me. He walked right up the steps and followed the woman into the house with the sure foot of someone who had been there before.

Chapter
10

"COME IN, MISS O'Neal. You must be dry from the heat."

I was standing there with my mouth open like an idiot, watching Sam follow Jackie into the house. Farrell's voice, the same low, hard voice I had heard on the phone, startled me. I nodded and walked up to the door. Farrell stood aside to let me pass.

The room was cool. My guess was that the tan stucco house was built with double walls, like a mission. Four-hundred-year-old technology that still works. The ceiling was low, with two circling fans, one over a conversation area that included a leather couch and two chairs set around a dark, heavy Mexican coffee table, wood bound with iron, the other over a pool table. The walls were mostly decorated with photographs of groups of men in uniform.

Farrell gestured toward the sofa with his three-fingered right hand.

"Have a seat."

"Where'd Sam go?"

"I suspect he and Jackie are in the kitchen. They'll be back in a minute."

"Did he tell you we were coming?" I was still standing just inside the door. I wasn't certain I wanted to sit.

"Did he lead you here?" Farrell countered.

"No. He said he was just along for the ride."

"Then why would he have called to say you were coming?"

"Oh, hell, I don't care why. I just want to know if he did."

"No. Sam didn't tell me you were coming. Now will you sit?"

"If I do, will you tell me what's going on?"

He shook his head. "I can't promise that. But I'll tell you a little about your father."

I sat on the leather couch, perched carefully on the edge of the cushion.

"I was hoping to avoid this." He moved to the coffee table, looked out the window over the sofa for a moment, then looked down at me. "Your daddy's dead. He has been for almost two years now."

Something inside me moved off center. I struggled to hold on to it, I didn't want to tilt in front of this deceptive old man. I should have expected him to say that, I should have been prepared. I should have worked out a long time ago how I'd feel if Danny were dead.

"Why should I believe you?"

My voice sounded alien, as if there wasn't any breath under it.

"Hell, honey, because it's true. That'd be an ugly thing for me to lie about."

"Yes. It would. But why didn't you just tell me over the phone?"

"Because it didn't seem right. And because I don't like to destroy hope."

We were eye to eye, and I was the one who looked away.

"We'll have a sandwich and a beer," he said, "and then I'll show you the grave."

"Here? Danny's buried here?"

"Well, he died here, and nobody seemed quite sure who to contact."

"Sam knew how to get hold of Mom." I was facing him again.

"I didn't know to ask Sam. And I guess I just didn't want to draw unnecessary attention to the place."

"You killed him. You, or somebody who works for you."

"We didn't have an autopsy done. But the unofficial cause of death was heart failure, brought on by acute alcohol poisoning. I believe you could say he killed himself."

"Goddamn you, you're lying!" I let it out unwisely, in one of those cries that explodes impossibly from the animal core.

"If you were a man, I'd teach you a lesson," Farrell said calmly, still looking down at me. "Since you're not much more than a girl, I'll let it go."

A rattle of dishes jerked us both toward the doorway that led into the interior of the house. Jackie was standing there, tray in hand, smiling at Farrell. Sam pushed past her, holding four open beer bottles between his fingers.

"Here you go, Freddie," he said, one arm outstretched.

"Thanks, Sam," I said, automatically taking the beer. I had to hold it with both hands.

Jackie put a tray with cold cuts, a loaf of sheepherder bread, mustard, mayonnaise, and utensils on the coffee table and settled herself on the floor in front of it.

"Help yourself," she said.

"Thanks, but I don't think I'm hungry," I whispered.

Sam sat in the chair next to the sofa and took a long swallow of beer.

"I'm sorry," he said.

"For what?" I didn't look at him.

"For not thinking that Jackie would be out here, or that Farrell might know what happened to Danny. I could have saved you some work. I'm also sorry Danny's gone and you didn't get to talk with him."

"You didn't know?"

"Not until Jackie just told me. If I'd known when you tracked me down in Virginia City, I would have said so."

I wanted to believe him, but I was too upset to sort things out. And I was frightened that he seemed to have accepted the story of Danny's death so easily.

"How'd you know about this place?"

"I came out here once with a friend who had some business with Farrell. Not Danny."

I glanced at Farrell and he nodded.

"So why didn't you just tell me, bring me straight here when you heard where we were going?"

This time Sam glanced at Farrell, who waited.

"Because I don't think your being here is a good idea, and I didn't want to help you find it." He paused, then added, "Although I didn't try to stop you."

"Does anybody want to tell me what's going on out here?" I looked from Sam to Farrell and back.

"No," Farrell answered. "Nobody wants to do that."

Jackie had fixed a sandwich for Farrell, who took it and sat in the other chair. Sam started fixing one for himself. I couldn't find my appetite.

"How far is the grave?" I asked.

Farrell chewed a moment before answering.

"Not far. There's a small cemetery in the foothills."

"Yeah. Sudden alcohol poisoning must be a real hazard around here."

This time he didn't say anything about my not being a man, but I knew he was thinking it. I decided to watch my mouth. I don't like getting weird breaks from men based on my sex.

Jackie had fixed another sandwich, and she held it out to me.

"I know you're not hungry," she said. "But it might make you feel better if you eat something."

Because I had just decided to watch what I said, I didn't comment on the Mom theory of comfort. I just shook my head. And for the first time noticed Jackie's eyes. They were blue and wide-set and lightly rimmed with blue mascara, but what caught my attention was the effort it took for her to focus them. Either this wasn't Jackie's first beer of the day, or she was using it to wash down tranquilizers.

"Half?" she asked hopefully.

I gave in, even though I didn't much want it.

"Thanks."

She cut it in half. I took one piece from her, she took a slow, small bite of the other. When I finally tried the sandwich, the texture of the bread felt wrong in my mouth, and the cold cuts seemed slimy and alien. The sound of my own chewing crackled in my ears. I put the sandwich down on a paper napkin.

"It seems to me," I said, looking from Jackie to Farrell, "that the two of you could fill in a lot about Danny, why he left Reno, where he went, how he ended up here, without compromising whatever's going on here in any way. And I would appreciate it a lot if you would do that."

Jackie wasn't going to talk without permission. Farrell nodded.

"I only knew him the last couple of months—I met him when he first came to town, right before he went to work for the Branding Iron. He seemed like a nice guy, but he sure did drink a lot." It was another Mom move, a trying-to-please-everybody stab.

"Oh, come on." I forgot I was going to watch my tongue. "He left Reno because he knew who killed my son, and he got scared." Farrell sounded more like he was ordering than explaining.

"Why?"

"He was working in a chop shop—a place where they disassemble stolen cars for the parts—and he thought he was in trouble no matter what he did, whether he kept quiet and the killer got him, or talked and the cops got him."

"Who was the killer?"

"That ain't part of the story."

It was easier, now that Farrell was sitting, to meet his eyes. Which were black and focused. No drink or drugs there.

"Danny should have come to me at the time," Farrell continued. "I would have protected him. He ran instead. He didn't come to me until two years ago, and then it was too late."

"Too late how?"

"Oh, hell, honey, hard living. He would have been a good candidate for a liver transplant, if the rest of his organs had been any good. I gave him a job, did what I could. He just didn't make it. If you didn't look so much like him, I'd think your mom had pulled a fast one. Wherever you got your backbone, it wasn't from him."

I knew it was supposed to be a compliment. I just didn't like it much.

"Whenever you're ready, I'd like to see the grave," was all I said.

Sam had a second sandwich by then, and I think he would have gotten himself a second beer if I hadn't been sitting there looking so miserable. It was after two by the time the three of us—Sam, Farrell, and me—got into the red pickup and wound through the buildings to the dirt road that led into the foothills to the north. Jackie stayed to do the dishes or something.

Until we got there, I was hoping that the whole thing would turn out to be some obvious kind of fraud, that Farrell would take me to a mound of freshly turned earth, or a marker with the paint still wet, the work of a hired hand done while we were held by food and drink. But about three miles out of the valley we rounded a curve and I saw the graveyard, a makeshift Boot Hill on a plateau facing west.

Farrell didn't bother to pull off the road before he turned off the engine. The sun was beating on us as we got out of the truck.

"Over there," Farrell said, pointing toward an area where the markers seemed newer. I walked beside him, passing a couple of stone angels I would have stopped to look at under other circumstances, until he stopped in front of a wooden cross. Somebody had burned in the crossbar "Daniel O'Neal" and a date of death. That was all. The ground was packed and the wood was weathered, as if it had been there for a while.

Everything was blurred. I wasn't sure what I felt. I tried to make some kind of connection between that marker and the father I vaguely remembered, and I couldn't do it. I thought about not looking for him anymore, not waiting for him any longer, and I didn't know how to do that.

"Okay," I said. "Thanks." I turned and started walking back to the truck. My foot slipped on a loose stone, and Sam caught my arm, harshly, pulling me up. For a second I almost leaned against him.

Farrell started the truck in silence.

"Who else is buried there?" I asked as we rode down the hill.

"A couple of miners from a long time ago, a couple of people from my family, nobody you'd know," Farrell answered.

That was all we had to say.

Coming into the compound from the north, I saw something that oddly hadn't registered from the other side. An airstrip, and a parking area with cement blocks where planes could tie down. Only one was there at the moment, a restored Navion. I could have flown the Cherokee in, and then I wouldn't have that motorcycle trip back to Las Vegas, and Moira and Doc, still ahead of me before I could go home. I wanted to ask Farrell about the Navion, and who used the airstrip, but I didn't feel cheerful enough to break the silence.

He parked the pickup next to the two Harleys.

"Do you want to come in?" he asked. "Have a cup of tea or something?"

What I didn't want was these two men feeling sorry for me. An ache was radiating out from the left side of my chest, up to my head and down into my hands and feet, and I needed to be alone for a minute.

"I'd just like to use the rest room before we leave, if that's okay," I said.

Farrell nodded, and the three of us trooped to the front door.

"Down the hall, first door to the left," Farrell said.

I walked carefully across the main room to the hall, found the first door to the left, and entered a closetlike room with a toilet and sink. I turned on the cold water and plunged my face into a double handful. It didn't help enough. I sat down on the tile floor and leaned my head against my knees.

Someone knocked gently on the door.

"Freddie? Are you all right?"

A woman's voice.

I struggled to say something.

"Freddie?"

"Just a minute!"

I grabbed the sink and pulled myself up, splashed more cold water on my face, and opened the door.

Jackie reached up and touched my wet cheek.

"It's okay," she said, looking at me with unfocused blue eyes. "If you want, you could lie down for a while before you start back. You could even stay the night, leave in the morning."

My body jerked erect at the thought.

"No," I told her. "Thank you. But I think we ought to go."

"I'm sorry," she said, shaking her head. "So sorry."

"About what?"

"Just sorry. About all of it."

She turned away, and I followed her back to the main room.

"I'm ready. Let's go," I said to Sam.

Sam got up off the couch and offered his hand to Farrell, who took it. I hated both of them for being alive.

"Thanks for your trouble" was what I said.

"No problem," Farrell replied.

I headed out the door, down the steps, and over to Moira's Harley without waiting for Sam. He was calling something to me as I turned the key and stepped on the gas, but I figured he could catch up.

He was next to me before I got out of the compound, gesturing for me to stop. I shook my head and went on. A covered transport truck was coming slowly down the hill, and I would have waited for it if I hadn't been upset. But there was room between the truck and the slope. I revved the engine, downshifted, and passed it. Once at the top of the hill, I had to pause at the gate, but only long enough for the guard to lift the arm, already down after the truck came through. I couldn't hear what Sam was saying, but I knew he was still shouting.

The trip back was a dreary one, hot, dusty, and relentless.

Sam tapped insistently on his gas gauge as we neared Indian Springs, and while I was pretty certain we could have made it all the way without refueling, I didn't object. I also didn't talk to him. I started my engine as soon as it had gas in it and moved back to the edge of the highway.

It was getting close to five when we reached North Las Vegas, and the traffic was picking up. I followed Sam off the highway, and we took surface streets for the last few miles. I didn't like it. The motorcycle was harder to handle in the stop-and-go traffic, and I was tired.

My ears were ringing and my whole body was stiff by the time the Harley was safely parked in the driveway behind the Winnebago. I wanted to hand Sam the key and leave, but my flight bag was still in the house.

"What happened?" Moria asked from the doorway.

"Danny's dead," Sam answered. "We saw the grave."

Moira moved aside and I stumbled past her into the living room, trying to remember where I had left my bag.

"Thanks for letting me ride your Harley," I said. "I'll just get my things and be off."

"Don't be silly. You can hardly walk." Even Mom couldn't have snapped it any better. "Take a shower, have something to eat, get a good night's sleep, and you can leave in the morning."

I didn't want to stay, but I didn't have enough energy to fight with her. And I wanted a shower and a nap more than anything in the world.

"Does somebody have a robe I can borrow?" There wasn't room in my flight bag for a robe, and I hadn't worried about that when I packed it, since I thought I'd be going right back.

"Toss me your clothes and I'll hand you one," she said.

I went into the bathroom, took my things off, and exchanged them for an old gray terry-cloth robe. I knew without asking that shirt, jeans, and underwear were headed straight for the washing machine. The hot water felt good, but it sapped what little strength I had left.

Moira was standing in the hall waiting as I opened the door.

"This way," she said. "I'll wake you when dinner's here. Doc's picking up some Chinese." She led me to one of the bedrooms. I was so tired I fell asleep without looking around.

The light was gray when I woke up. A digital clock next to the bed showed 7:13, and I couldn't tell if it was A.M. or P.M. I was still in the gray bathrobe, but someone had tossed a quilt over me. Lucky Lucy was curled up in the bend of my knees. I decided it had to be morning, because my clothes were neatly folded on a chair in front of a vanity, and I was starved.

The bedroom belonged to a woman, not just because of the vanity and its perfume bottles, which were something I wouldn't have expected Moira to collect, but because of the lily-of-the-valley quilt, and the framed Georgia O'Keefe poster, and the vase of dried purple statice on the dresser. The heavy boots outside the closet door could have been anybody's. I considered looking inside the closet, but then I didn't want to.

I sat up, waking Lucky Lucy, who stretched good-naturedly, hopped off the bed, and waited for me to open the bedroom door and let her out. I got dressed first. We could go out together.

The smell of coffee and frying bacon hit my nose and reminded me again that I had slept through dinner. Lucky Lucy trotted down the hall, and I followed her. Doc was alone in the kitchen, fixing breakfast.

"Hey, Freddie," he said.

"Hey, Doc."

"Pour yourself some coffee. How many strips of bacon do you want?"

"A couple will do." My mouth was watering and my stomach gurgling. I got a mug out of the cupboard and filled it with coffee, something warm to hold me.

"I have some pancake batter here. Do you want pancakes?" He peeled three more strips of bacon from the rasher and tossed them onto a griddle, moving the strips already there toward the edge.

"Sure. That would be fine." I thought about the way people kept trying to feed me, and how it echoed the fine old American custom of bringing casseroles to the grieving family. And it was the one thing I was certain I would miss when I was home alone.

"Did you sleep okay?"

"Yeah."

"Moira should be up soon, I don't know about Sam. Moira tried to wake you for dinner last night, but you were sleeping so soundly she gave up, figured you needed it."

"Probably she was right."

"There's a pitcher of orange juice in the refrigerator." He turned the bacon, again rearranging the strips. "I heard about your father. I'm sorry."

"Yeah, okay, thanks." I poured myself some orange juice, and the ache started radiating again. "It's been so long since I've seen him, it really doesn't matter much."

"'After the first death, there is no other,'" Doc said.

"What?"

"Dylan Thomas."

"That's right, you teach English."

"Yes. And I have an eight o'clock Modern Literature class." He lifted the bacon from the griddle and set the strips on a paper towel. Then he ladled out batter, smoothing it into neat circles. I got hungrier as I watched, waiting for the little bubbles so he could flip them. The ache in my stomach was overpowering the one in my chest. Doc handed me the plates, refilled his coffee cup, and sat down opposite me at the small table. "What time do you plan on leaving?"

"Right after breakfast."

"Without saying good-bye to Moira or Sam?"

"I'll leave a note." I drizzled syrup over the short stack.

"I know you're not sure who's a friend and who isn't right now, but we care about you. And you might want to remember that before you get rude."

His voice was gentle, and the bite of pancake he forked into his mouth took the edge off what he said.

"I'll leave a polite note," I said.

The truth was that I didn't want to see either of them, and I wouldn't have stayed for breakfast if I hadn't been too hungry to walk out the door. I was rude, of course—Doc's Harley was loud enough to wake the whole block, and the note that I left on the telephone before I dashed out the door just thanked them for their hospitality and said I'd be in touch.

I drove to the airport as fast as I could, irrationally afraid that somebody would try to stop me. I didn't relax until I had done the walkaround, strapped myself into the Cherokee, and asked for clearance to take off. The surge from the engine just before the plane lifted snapped all the nerves in my body back into place.

My flight plan took me just east of Beatty, and I thought about a short detour over Farrell's outpost. I didn't do it, both because I wanted to get home and because for all I knew he had an antiaircraft gun in one of the buildings.

I was looking forward to Reno, I felt as if I had been gone for a month, but the Indian summer had broken overnight, and the day stayed gray, and Cannon International Airport looked worn and uninviting. I tied down at the small charter terminal, avoided Jerry McIntire, who was always behind the counter, and drove home.

I cheered up a little walking through the door. No carnage greeted me, either because Deke had kept the cats well fed or because he had cleaned up the traces. Or almost. Butch and Sundance were both asleep on the bed, until I startled them awake, and as I tossed my flight bag onto the chair I saw something dark on the carpet in front of it. Batwings, with little claws hooked to the shag. Cats aren't supposed to be able to catch bats, but Butch gets them on the swoop. I had to remember to check when his rabies booster was due. Both cats decided my entrance wasn't worth commenting on and fell back asleep.

The light had been flashing on my answering machine, and I went back to the office to check. Mom. Shit. I would have to call Mom and tell her about Danny. And Sandra. And there was a message from an Officer Maddox, asking me to call him. Maddox. I had to think to remember who he was.

And then I remembered Gary Hanrahan.

Chapter
11

MADDOX HAD CALLED to let me know that he was at a dead end on the Hanrahan case and to remind me that I had promised to share anything I found out. I told him I remembered my promise, but I had nothing to share. And that was sort of true—since Danny had died two years ago, my investigation had nothing to do with Gary Hanrahan, who had been shot for some other reason, not because he had some information for me about Danny. Still, I wished I had asked Jared Farrell about Hanrahan, even though he would have either denied knowledge or told me it was none of my business. I wasn't certain what my business was anymore.

After a suitably long period of deliberation, ending in a total inability to think of any excuse not to, I picked up the phone and called Mom.

"Danny's dead," I told her. "I saw the grave."

There was a long, uncharacteristic pause.

"Are you okay?" I asked.

"Oh, yes. It's just that he'll never be able to sign the divorce papers now."

I controlled the flare of anger that burned down to my fingertips. "It doesn't matter, Mom. You're a widow, and maybe you can talk Al into marrying you all over again, to celebrate your anniversary or something."

"What a good idea! We could do it right after the election, take a vacation and get married again."

"After the election? I thought you were worried about someone rattling the skeleton before the election."

"Well, it isn't bigamy any longer, just a technicality. That's not nearly as bad. Do you want to come this time? I always thought your not coming to the wedding was the big reason you and Al never hit it off."

"No, I don't want to come, and there are a raft of reasons why Al and I never hit it off. None of them have changed."

"Something has changed. Danny's dead. It's time you stopped resented Al for not being Danny."

"I'll think about it."

I hung up as quickly as I could without being too rude to Mom. I hadn't expected her to go into mourning—she thinks black makes her look too pale. I guess I had just wanted her to be a little sympathetic. And that hadn't even occurred to her.

I was about to go vent my anger in a workout when the phone rang.

"I'm sorry," Mom said. "I didn't think until I got off the phone, but of course you're upset about Danny. You did a wonderful job tracking him down, and I didn't even congratulate you for it, and you found him dead. That had to have been hard for you. I'll be there in an hour. We can have an early dinner and you can tell me the whole story. We'll talk about old times—a private wake for Danny O'Neal."

I thought about telling her not to come. But I was touched that she realized, even belatedly, that Danny was more than a technicality to me. I also thought that she had once loved him a lot.

"Just the two of us?"

"Just the two of us," she said.

"Okay. See you."

Butch had hopped up on the desk while I was talking. I tucked him under my arm, ignoring his squeak of outrage, and walked back to the bedroom, forgetting I was going to work out. I wanted to lie down and think while I was waiting for Mom. I had thought about having dinner with Deke, but I appreciated the fact that Mom was willing to leave Al for the evening and feed me. The American way of grief. Let somebody feed you as long as you can.

I lay down on the bed and let Butch dance on my chest while I scratched the base of his spine. Sundance yawned, stretched, and recurled himself next to my shoulder. I told him Mom was coming, and he purred.

The thing was, I felt like a failure, finding Danny, but finding him dead. I could have searched for him two years earlier, I could have decided to look for him when I got out of college, I could have found him alive if I had only started sooner and tried harder. I might even have made a difference in his life. And discovering that he had left Reno because of a murder, not because of Mom and me, didn't make me feel better. After all, he still wanted to leave us—he could have gotten in touch, and he didn't, and now he could never tell me he was sorry. No matter what I did, no matter how hard I tried, Danny was never going to love me. Because he was dead.

I was still lying mired in self-pity when I heard the knocker on the front door pounding. It was a painful sound. I ought to install a doorbell.

Sundance knew it was Mom. I don't know how he senses it, but if it's anybody else, he stays in the bedroom. This time he trotted ahead of me to the door.

"Where do you want to go?" she asked, picking up a purring cat.

"What you see is what you get," I said, gesturing at my jeans and sweatshirt. Not that she was dressed for Eugene's, or any place chic like that. She was wearing a variation of her signature denim with spangles. "Where do you want to take me?"

"If you'll just put on a clean shirt and brush your hair, we can go to the Comstock Room."

I figured I could do that much.

"We'll take my car," I said.

I would have walked, normally, since the Comstock Room was the restaurant on the top floor of the Mother Lode Casino, whose coffee shop was my usual dining spot. But Mom wouldn't make it that far in her stiletto heels, and I had decided some time ago that I wouldn't ride with her again until she got glasses. How she got her driver's license renewed without them was beyond me.

I parked in the Center Street lot, and we worked our way across the alley full of tourists to the casino. The elevator to the Comstock Room was about midway between the Center and Virginia entrances, but Mom couldn't make it that far without pulling out a handful of quarters.

"This one looks lucky," she said, stopping at a slot machine.

Deke and Sandra have both told me I'm the only person who grew up in Reno who gambles. Actually, there are two of us. The difference is that I play Keno and Mom plays the quarter slots. That's one difference. The other difference is that she wins.

Three cherries came up on her first coin, and Mom paused while the quarters clinked into the cup.

"Do you want some?" she asked.

"No. I'd only lose them."

"You'll lose them if you think you will. I'll just be a minute."

Mom was one of those people for whom Norman Vincent Peale spoke revealed truth. I didn't time it, but I think it took her about a minute and a half to win a fifty-dollar jackpot. She took the bells and whistles and flashing red lights as her due, applause for the tough work of dropping coins in a slot, and smiled graciously at the thin young woman with frizzed brown hair, wearing fishnet stockings and change apron, who paid her and reset the machine and didn't smile back.

"Let's go," she said, stuffing rolls of quarters in her purse. "We can play more after dinner."

The elevator opened into a red velvet foyer with a crystal chandelier that would have made Julia Bulette feel right at home. The decor in the Comstock Room was fake Virginia City and authentic bad taste. A plumed hostess ushered us to a small table near a west window. Eating early meant that we were going to get one of Reno's best views of the sunset.

The cocktail waitress, like the hostess, was dressed up as somebody's fantasy of a nineteenth-century hooker. She took Mom's order for a martini on the rocks and mine for a beer. A waiter wearing long pants and a red jacket gave us menus.

"To Danny," Mom said. "May his soul rest in peace."

"To Danny," I agreed, clinking my beer bottle against her martini glass.

"Now tell me how you found him."

I brought her up-to-date on Sam, Moira, and Doc, skirted around Jackie Ellis, and ended with the scene at Bullfrog. Before she could comment, the waiter arrived for our order. I ordered the prime rib rare. Mom could pay for it out of her winnings. She ordered lobster Newburg and another round of drinks.

"I'm glad Sam went with you," she said when the waiter had left.

"Why?"

"Because he can take care of himself, and he wouldn't have let anything happen to you."

I shrugged. "Maybe. But I don't like it that he didn't tell me he'd been there before. It made me wonder what else he didn't tell me."

Mom got a funny expression on her face.

"Or what else you're not telling me," I added.

"Nothing." She didn't give it her full snap, so I waited for her to continue. "I saw Sam once after Danny left, when I was trying to find him to get the divorce papers signed. Sam had always liked me, and under other circumstances we might have gotten together. But the time was never right, and we never did."

"Then why do I have an almost memory of seeing the two of you together? I can't pin it down, but there's something that happened a long time ago, before Danny left, that has to do with Sam."

Her expression got funnier.

"Sam came to see Danny once, unexpectedly, on a night when Danny didn't come home. He slept on the couch and left early in the morning. Your paths didn't cross, you were only about ten years old, you were asleep in your bedroom, and there's no reason for you to remember it."

"Yeah, okay. I won't push it. Did you ever meet Moira?"

Her expression went from funny to tight.

"Why?"

"I just wondered what you thought of her."

"I met her once at the camel races. And I think she is a very foolish woman for not marrying one of them, either one. Living that way is going to backfire sooner or later. That's what I think."

Mom stiff is even worse than Mom snappy.

"Mom? Are you sure you wouldn't have been happier with Sam than with Al?"

"This is a wake for Danny, not a critique of my marriage."

"You're right. I'm sorry." I had to ease up on her or we were going to have a fight over Al, and I didn't want to do that. "To Daniel O'Neal. An Irishman to the end."

I held up my beer bottle and waited for her to join me. She held up her glass.

"To James Joseph Daniel O'Neal the Fourth," she countered. "If you want to be formal."

"That was his name? Why didn't I know that?"

"You must have known. You just forgot, because he never used anything but Danny. His father had been Jimmy, and his mother didn't want to call him Joey, because she thought that sounded like a kangaroo, so he was Danny from the time he was a baby."

"Hell." I put the bottle down, forgetting to drink.

"What?"

"The marker. There's just a wood marker on his grave, it doesn't even have his date of birth, and the name's wrong. Probably he didn't know he was going to die, so he couldn't tell them."

The waiter arrived with salads. Iceberg lettuce with bottled French dressing, the all-American choice. He placed the second round of drinks discreetly behind the first, which we hadn't quite finished.

"That's too bad," Mom said. "A shame, really."

The waiter started to react, but Mom shook her head, letting him know she didn't mean him.

"Yeah, it's a shame."

Our salads were followed by the main course, my bloody prime rib and Mom's creamy lobster. And then we had cheesecake and coffee. And brandy. She told a few good Danny stories, about how he pitched winning softball games at telephone company picnics and sang all the verses to

"Street of Laredo" afterward, and how he spiked the punch at the Mary S. Doten PTA meeting, the one time she had talked him into coming with her. The sunset was a spectacular salute, and we were both pretty mellow by the time the check came.

She stumbled as we got up from the table.

"Are you sure you're okay to drive back to the lake?" I asked.

"I'm fine. And Al will be waiting for me."

She straightened herself up and we left.

I asked again when we got back to my place, but she still insisted she was fine, and she didn't want to come in for more coffee. I couldn't argue with that.

I was restless after she left, too much coffee, and brandy never does sit well with me, so I walked to the video store and rented three movies, no-brainers, but with strong women's roles. I'm getting to the point where I can't watch movies about passive women anymore. And it has really cut down my rentals.

I couldn't watch these movies anyway. I felt too bad to sit and watch movies. I left the house a little after eleven, in time to catch Deke at the Mother Lode before his shift started.

He was already in uniform when I found him.

"I need some advice," I said.

"I must have died and gone to heaven and not noticed," he said, staggering backward and clutching his heart. "What happened to you?"

I started to tell him the story, but he cut me off.

"Come on," he said. "I'm on duty. You have to walk with me."

In a strange way, it was easier to tell it because he wasn't looking at me. We were standing by the Virginia Street entrance, watching tourists pass through the air curtain, while I told him about Danny and Sam and Jared and Mom.

"So what do you want to do?" he asked when I had finished.

"I want to put a real marker, a stone marker, on his grave," I said.

"And you want my advice?" He shook his head. "Shit. You know my advice. Do it, girl. Just get the marker and do it."

I thanked him and left. Walking home I felt dumb. I should have known that was what he would say. I did know. I just wanted to hear somebody say it. I felt cold, too. And that made me feel even dumber, that I knew it was getting close to winter, and I didn't have sense enough to put on an extra layer of clothes. What a failure.

The next morning I looked up "Tombstones" in the Yellow Pages, only to be referred to "Memorial Tablets." I called the first name listed and said I wanted a marker for my father. The woman started to mumble some formulaic condolence, but I cut her off.

"He's been dead for two years," I said.

"Oh. Then it's time he had a memorial, isn't it? When can you come in?" she asked.

"Can't I just order something over the phone?"

"Certainly. We can send you our catalog, and you can choose size, style, inscription, and typeface, if coming to the shop isn't convenient. You can call when you've made your decision."

I hadn't thought about all that. I had just thought something plain and lasting, with name and dates.

"Okay. Do that." I gave her my name and address. "How long will it take?"

"If your father is interred locally, we can have the marker installed in about a month."

"He isn't, and I want to do it myself."

"The memorial tablet will be ready from two to three weeks after you place the order. We could call you."

"Fine." I figured that would be time enough. Danny had had the wooden cross for two years, he could wait a couple more weeks for something better.

After I hung up, I thought that maybe I should go to the shop, see real samples, not just catalog pictures. But I sat there. I had a fantasy of stumbling through a room of molded cement angels, hitting my head against wings. Catalog pictures were as close as I was willing to get. I've read enough to know that discomfort in the face of death is a cultural problem, but that doesn't make me immune.

I would have liked to do something more for Danny, except I couldn't think of anything he would have wanted. I even thought about having the body dug up and interred locally, as the woman had put it, but the grave seemed better placed out there in the desert, facing the sunset, than in some Reno cemetery. And I knew I wouldn't visit it, even if it were close. The marker was going to be good-bye.

When I picked it up, I would have to call Jared Farrell, let him know I was coming to put it on the grave, but that could wait. I didn't want to talk to him until I had to. And I'd have to think about whether to let Sam know, in case he wanted to be there, make it kind of a ceremony. Sam, Jared, Jackie, and me? Maybe Moira and Doc? It sounded awful. I would have to think of a way I could go alone. Unless Mom wanted to go, I would have to tell Mom.

I called, but she was short with me. Al was having another of his committee meetings, and she was getting more involved as the campaign progressed.

"I think what you're doing is wonderful, dear, and I'll be happy to pay for it, but I just don't think this is a good time for me to be gone," was what she said.

I had been shuffling through papers while I was on the

phone, and several had drifted to the floor. I picked them up, and the scrap with Maddox's number on it had settled on top. He hadn't exactly told me that the file on Hanrahan was closed, but he had certainly indicated that it wasn't a high priority unless they got a new lead. And it was still true that Hanrahan had been killed while on his way to meet me. I didn't have anything scheduled for the afternoon. Not only that, but finding that Danny was dead hadn't washed away the guilt I felt about the timing of Hanrahan's murder. I couldn't feel any worse, and making a few inquiries about Hanrahan might help me feel better.

Starting with the obvious, I checked the telephone book. Gary Hanrahan was listed, an address on Commercial Street, the ratty part of downtown, one of those blocks that spoils the view from high-rise hotels. Too far to walk.

I parked the Jeep in front of a run-down, two-story frame house that had been painted blue several winters ago. The tree in the fenced yard had either dropped its leaves early or given up and died in August. I climbed the four steps to the cement stoop and rang the bell.

I waited and rang again. A forest-green Hyundai was in the driveway, so somebody was most likely inside. The door was the old-fashioned kind, with a square window veiled in lace. A hand brushed it, then pulled the bolt.

"What?" A woman, maybe thirty, in a dirty yellow bathrobe, red hair hanging around her shoulders, still matted from the pillow, leaned around a crack in the door. Her skin was white and freckled, and traces of black mascara were smeared under her pale blue eyes.

"I'm sorry. I guess I woke you up." I flashed my PI license at her, too fast for her to see anything. She was bleary enough that I probably could have dangled it. "I'm looking for Gary Hanrahan."

"Why?"

"An insurance matter."

"Oh, for God's sake. Whatever it is, you're too late. He's dead, about a month ago."

"Were you his landlady?"

"No. I was his daughter."

"Oh, hell. Nobody told me he had a daughter."

She blinked. "So why do you care?"

"Because he was on his way to meet me the night somebody shot him."

She checked my face carefully as she let that sink in. "Come in. Give me a minute. I'll put some coffee on."

I followed her into a living room that had to have been furnished once-upon-a-time by her mother. Faded chintz tea roses covered a sofa and two matching armchairs. A coffee table and two end tables had glass tops and carved feet. An old upright piano took up most of the remaining space.

The woman gestured toward the sofa. "I'll be right back."

I caught a glimpse of more carved feet on a heavy table in a formal dining room before I sat. I heard some rattling from the kitchen, then silence. There was nothing to look at in the living room except the piano. Someone played it, not often enough to leave the keys exposed, but often enough to leave a worn book of *Bach's Greatest Hits* on the bench.

More rattling in the kitchen preceded the woman's return. She had brushed her hair and dressed, in jeans and a ruffled poet's shirt the same pale blue as her eyes. She placed a mug of black coffee on the table in front of me and held on to another as she sat in one of the chairs. The ruffles on her sleeves fell back, exposing fleshless wrists below long, thin hands. Her span had to be more than an octave, ten keys easy.

"I didn't think to ask if you wanted anything in it." She said it without apology, as if I might be out of luck if I did want anything in my coffee. "Now, who are you and why was my father meeting you?"

"I'm Freddie O'Neal, I'm a private investigator, and your father was meeting me because he had some information about my father, who is also dead."

She looked at me as if she thought I might be lying. I knew it sounded like an attempt to establish some kind of fake rapport, but I couldn't help it if we had dead fathers in common.

"At the door you said it was an insurance matter."

"I didn't know who you were, and I had to say something."

That didn't help.

I pulled out my license again, this time handing it to her.

"Okay," she said, handing it back. "You're a private investigator. Go on."

"I was looking for my father, Danny O'Neal. Your father said he might have some information for me, promised to meet me. He never made it. I found him in his truck. I haven't followed up on his death before because I didn't want to get in Officer Maddox's way, and I wasn't sure it had anything to do with his meeting with me in any case. But this afternoon I had an irresistible impulse to see where Gary Hanrahan had lived."

"Fine. So you've seen it." She was still skeptical. "Why were you looking for your dad if he's dead?"

"I didn't know he was dead then. I just found out a couple of days ago."

"Where did our dads know each other?"

"Danny was a bartender at the Old Corral, years ago."

"The place where my dad drank."

"Right."

"But you say you found your dad, or found out he's dead.

So I still don't understand why you're here. The irresistible impulse, as you called it."

The pale blue eyes were cold and hard. I hadn't made a good impression.

"Probably the best answer is that I feel guilty. I've been afraid your father was shot because he was meeting me, and I feel guilty about that, and the only way I know how to stop feeling guilty is to see if I can't find out who killed him and why and make certain it was about something else."

She put the coffee mug down. "I couldn't help the officer, and I don't know how I can help you. Dad didn't have any enemies, or any friends for that matter, except for the people he drank with. During the day he mostly hung around the house. Sometimes he did odd jobs. I work nights, and he drank at the bar. That's it."

The implication was that I'd have to feel better on my own.

"Where do you work?" I said it as pleasantly as I could, ignoring the fact that she was clearly ready for me to leave.

"Washoe Cab. I drive a taxi." She said it flatly. My stab at warm and friendly hadn't changed her lousy impression of me.

"Look. I might be able to help. I'd like to try. So if you could at least go over your conversation with Officer Maddox, it would give me a place to start."

She shrugged. "Maddox wanted to know about friends and enemies, what Dad had done the last day or two, whether anything unusual had happened. I told him Dad was a solitary man who watched television and drank. The same thing I told you."

"Did you check your telephone bill? That might have come in after you talked to Maddox. Were there any strange calls?"

"There was one." The woman leaned forward, tilting her

head to get a better look at me. "I thought maybe it was a mistake. It was a call to one of the ghost towns, Bullfrog, made the day before Dad died."

"Thanks." I fished a card out of my pocket and placed it on the coffee table next to my mug. "If you think of anything else, please call me."

"That means something to you, Bullfrog. What?"

"For one thing, it's where Danny is buried."

"And for another?"

"I don't know yet. Do you know any of the Farrells—Cliff or Jared or any other member of the family?"

"No. Why?"

"They're the link between Bullfrog and the Old Corral. And your father evidently knew them both."

"Dad never mentioned them."

I stood. "Thanks for the coffee."

"You really do want to help, don't you?"

I didn't answer. I just waited.

"What did your dad die of?" she asked.

"Alcohol poisoning, they told me, but I didn't see any autopsy report."

"Tough. I'm sorry." She walked with me to the door. "Next time call before you come over."

"If I do, who do I ask for?"

"Maudie." In answer to my unspoken question she added, "For Maud Gonne."

I held out my hand and she took it. Hers was less fragile than I would have guessed.

"I'll call when I know something."

As I drove home, I thought about calling Maddox, but I decided I didn't really have anything to tell him. And anyway, I didn't want him to reopen the Hanrahan file just yet. I wanted to ask Jared Farrell about Hanrahan myself.

Chapter
12

THE INFORMATION ON the memorial tablets arrived two days later. It wasn't really a catalog—just some photocopied pages of rectangles with different kinds of inscriptions and a price list. Bibles, rosaries, and Masonic symbols were available, but no angels. No grim reapers, either.

Nothing in it changed my mind. I called the woman at the shop and told her what I wanted. His name, dates of birth and death, plain block letters.

"What about 'Beloved Father'?" she asked.

"I don't think so. Name and dates will do it."

She read it back to me, spelling the name, and added "Beloved Father."

"Name and dates," I said. "That's it. And I want it embedded in a stone, like a historical marker."

I just couldn't deal with "Beloved Father." Maybe if he had died in Vietnam. I had yet another twinge of guilt—they were becoming as regular as heartbeats—wishing for a moment that Danny had died in Vietnam a hero, years before he had come home and then left us.

"Most cemeteries don't allow raised tablets," she said. "They want them flat. It's easier to keep up the grounds that way."

"This one's a little different."

"You'll have to come in and pick out a stone."

"I'll tell you what—I'll find the one I want and bring it to you."

After I hung up I tried to come up with a suitable place to pick out a stone. I thought about Virginia City and Pyramid Lake, sites heavy with history. I thought about the Old Corral.

It was still light when I got there, too early for the bar to be open. I parked the Jeep in the lot and scrambled up the slope behind the building. I didn't have to spend much time looking around to realize this wasn't going to work. Anything I could lift was going to be too soft or too crumbly. I dug in my heels and half walked, half slid back to the parking lot.

Hardy McCullen was waiting for me.

"What's going on?" he asked.

"I'm looking for a stone."

"Well, there are plenty around."

"It has to be the right stone." I had to tell him, but it still wasn't easy to talk about. "I found my father. He's dead. I'm having a marker made for his grave, and I want it embedded in stone."

"I'm sorry—"

"It's okay." I cut him off. I didn't want sympathy, and that was all he could offer.

"Can I help you find what you're looking for?"

"Well, maybe we could walk along the road a little."

We started along the shoulder, headed north.

"How'd you find him?" McCullen asked.

"You gave me the key—and it's time I came out here and thanked you. He's buried near Bullfrog, on Jared Farrell's land. The old man said Danny knew who killed his son, and that's why he ran all those years ago. He came back just in time to die."

"Then your questions didn't have anything to do with Hanrahan's death?"

"I just don't know about that." I stopped and looked at him. I wasn't sure how much I could trust him. "But with Danny dead for two years, I guess none of the rest of it is my business."

"Sure." He seemed puzzled. I started walking again.

"There." I pointed at a rock about two and a half feet high, three feet across, with a textured sloping top, and maybe some quartz or pyrite crystals in it, because something glittered where the setting sun hit it. "That one will do."

"Get your Jeep," McCullen said. "I'll help you load it."

He waited while I brought the Jeep around. It took both of us to maneuver the stone into the back of the Jeep.

"Thanks," I said. "It was nice of you to help me."

"No problem." He waited until I was about to start the car and then added, "I really am sorry that your search didn't have a happier ending. And I hope you stop by for a beer some evening, just anytime you feel like it."

"Thanks again." I didn't plan on it, but it was nice of him to ask.

The next day I drove the stone to the memorial tablet place. I was disappointed to discover that there was no yard full of molded cement angels after all. In fact, it was just a storefront on East Fourth Street, with some kind of a workroom in back.

The woman I had talked with turned out to be in her fifties, gray-haired and still disapproving because I hadn't wanted "Beloved Father" on the marker. She commandeered two men from the workroom to get the stone from the back of the Jeep and said she would call when it was ready.

Three days later I was sitting in my office once again killing computerized Klingons and getting on with my life when I heard the unmistakable roar of a Harley. The engine stopped in my driveway. Butch jumped off my desk, scattering pages as he fled. When the pounding started on the door, I thought about not answering, but I knew he had to have seen the Jeep.

"Hello, Sam," I said as I opened the door.

He was dusty enough to have come all the way from Vegas without stopping.

"Aren't you going to ask me in? Let me wash up? Offer me a beer?"

I thought about saying no. But I stepped back from the door. "Least I can do," I said. "Your first stop is the end of the hall."

He was still damp when he came back, as if he had stuck his head under the faucet and not dried it very well. I had gotten the beers from the refrigerator and brought them back to my office. I wanted to keep the meeting formal, and, I hoped, short.

Sam took a beer and sat in one of the canvas chairs across from the desk. I stayed standing.

"Come on," he said. "Sit. You can't be that upset about seeing me."

"I'm not exactly thrilled," I said. "And I'll sit on one condition. Tell me what you know about Jared Farrell."

"Fine. I planned to. I wanted to make things right between us, and that was the only thing I thought might work."

"Nothing to make right." I sat in my big, cracked leather chair.

"Sure there is. We went riding together, and then you

didn't even want to say good-bye." He waited for me to comment on that, and when I didn't, he continued. "You got to stop being afraid every man is going to betray your trust, just because Danny did."

"I just don't see that's your business."

"It ain't. But I like you, and I think it's too bad you hurt yourself this way."

"Back off," I said. "Tell me what you came to say about Farrell."

"He's an arms dealer. Has been for years."

"Smuggles guns to the IRA?"

"Among others. Also the Contras, Iran and Iraq, and whoever's paying him in the Balkans. He was the employer of last resort for every shaky vet who had trouble landing a peacetime job. The family-owned bars were a cover business, so nobody would question some low-key prosperity. Danny didn't have the stomach for the arms deals, and even though I knew he'd tended bar before, I swear to you I didn't think he'd turn to Farrell when he said he wanted to stop running."

"Do you also swear you didn't know what he was running from?"

"I think he would have told me if I'd gone with him to Mexico—and maybe I should have gone. But I didn't go, and he didn't talk."

"Okay. What else have you got to say?"

"Not much. Just that I know this has been tough on you, and I hoped we could get past it and be friends."

"I don't know, Sam. I just don't know." I knew he had gone way out of his way to tell me that, and I was touched. But he had hit home when he said I didn't trust men. And I wasn't sure I should start with him.

He finished his beer and put the can on my desk.

"I'll probably be around for a day or two. Thought I

might stop by and say hello to Ramona, just for old times' sake. That is, if you'll let me know how to get in touch with her."

The thought of Al opening the door and finding Sam appealed to something perverse in me. I gave him directions to the Tahoe house.

Mom called early that evening.

"How could you?" she asked.

"How could I what?"

"Encourage Sam to come here. The whole thing was awkward. And you knew it would be."

"Yeah. I just wanted to anyway."

"Whatever was behind it, I'm glad you did."

"Why?"

"It seems you neglected to tell Sam that you were going back to Bullfrog to put a marker on Danny's grave. The three of us—Sam and Al and I—agreed that it's too dangerous for you to go alone. Sam should go with you."

Shit. Hoist on my own petard.

"I don't want Sam to go with me. He'll probably want to bring Moira and Doc, and it'll be awful."

"You'll have to discuss that with him. He's on his way back to Reno, and I think he was heading straight to your place."

I heard the Harley less than an hour later. I thought about leaving, but it would only have postponed the inevitable. He would have been waiting on the porch when I got back.

"What the hell do you think you're planning?" he said when I opened the door. A heavy leather jacket and leather chaps covered his vest and jeans. The night was cold. Reno was going to see frost by November.

"Not a damn thing that concerns you," I answered.

"After what I told you, I thought you'd know better'n to go back there."

"I'm doing the right thing. And you know it."

I was blocking the doorway. No way was he getting in.

"If Danny had died and got buried someplace else, going back with a marker would be the right thing. Not there. Jared Farrell let you come and go once, he might not do it again."

"Oh, hell. What's he going to do?"

"Nothing, as long as you let him alone. But he won't want to be messed with, and going back might look like messing with him."

"Thanks for the warning. I'll work it out with him when I get there."

Sam leaned forward against the doorjamb. I might have felt threatened if he'd been taller.

"I'm going with you, whether you like it or not. If you don't let me in, I'll just camp here in your yard till you're ready to leave."

I had known the resentment was building. I've been taking care of myself for too many years to want to share the task. But the sense that he might actually do that, camp in my yard, pushed me over the edge.

"Get out of my life," I shouted. "You're too old, too fat, you live in a weird situation, you probably slept with my mother, and I don't want anything to do with you." I would have slammed the door if his hand hadn't been in the way.

I didn't expect him to laugh. When he did, I felt stupid.

"I'm too old and too fat to deal with what you just said, that's for sure." He raised both hands and stepped back in a gesture of surrender. "I think you're making a mistake. I hope you change your mind. I'll be in touch, and you can let me know."

I stood on the porch and watched him ride away, part of me wishing I hadn't lost my temper, even though I meant what I said. I didn't want anything to do with him.

When the woman from Memorial Tablets called to let me know the marker was ready, I still hadn't heard from Sam. I was mostly relieved.

I thought about taking the Cherokee, but if I flew, I was going to have to call Jared Farrell before I left, and then he might have objections to my violating his airspace. Better to show up with the stone in the back of the Jeep.

My plan was to pick up the stone, drive to Bullfrog, place it on the grave at sunset, make my good-byes, spend the night at a motel in Beatty, and drive back the next morning. No need to even ask Deke to feed the cats.

The morning was cool, but I still picked up a bottle of water to take with me in the Jeep. You never know about the desert.

The same two men who had unloaded the stone loaded it back again. The stone still glittered in the sun, the bronze plaque looked fine on it, and I felt I had made a good choice.

The woman put it on my credit card, biting her lip to keep from mentioning that I was a lousy human being because I hadn't ordered "Beloved Father." Hell. He was a lousy human being.

I was on the road before noon, with no word from or sign of Sam. Beatty was six hours of desolate driving away, with only short stops, and I was tired of the desert by the time I hit Fallon. Fallon actually is farming country, because of irrigation from Lahontan Dam, but it's hard to tell that in October. At Fallon I turned south on Highway 95, through the Walker River Indian Reservation, past Walker Lake to Hawthorne.

I stopped in Hawthorne to stretch my legs, not because I had to, but because I wanted to head off a possible stop in Tonopah. I had a bad experience there once, and I didn't want to renew the memory.

Tonopah and Goldfield are both former mining centers,

like Beatty. And they're in the mountains, a break from the desert. I'm not sure how those old nineteenth-century miners knew when to stop moving and start digging. Maybe there were so many of them swarming across the state that somebody stuck a shovel in the ground every few miles. And actually, Tonopah and Goldfield were both part of the second boom, right at the turn of the century. It didn't last long.

There's something sad about both towns now, the way there is about Virginia City, but worse. Tonopah has some military presence, but Goldfield doesn't even have that. And neither town has many tourists. One of these days I ought to find out what keeps them going.

Driving into Beatty from the north was just like coming up from the south. I only knew I was there because of the sign and then the one blinking red light at the junction where I turned west to Bullfrog.

The sun was nearing the mountaintops when I bounced off the highway and onto the private road near the red barn antiques place. Those heavy trucks were hard on the road, and it would have made sense to pave it. Also would have drawn attention to it, though. I stopped at the gate and waited for the guard. It was the same young man.

"Mr. Farrell didn't tell me you were coming," he said.

"I guess he forgot."

"I'll have to check with him." He retreated into the small building and came back a moment later. "Mr. Farrell says this isn't a good time for you to come in. I guess you forgot to tell him you were coming."

"Try again. Tell him I don't want to stay. I just came to put a stone marker on Danny's grave, and then I'll turn around and leave."

He was looking pretty dubious. And I don't know that Farrell would have let me in. Except that two of those covered trucks loomed behind me, and I had no place to go but forward. The guard waved at the driver of the first one and retreated to the hut again. He was on the phone a little longer this time. Then the crossarm rose.

I might have tried to bypass the house and go straight to the grave, but there was no good way to go around it without getting close enough to see anyone standing on the front steps. And Farrell was out there motioning me to pull up next to him. I did, and he got in.

"What the hell do you think you're doing?" he asked.

"Just putting a proper marker on my old daddy's grave," I told him.

He glanced at the stone in the back of the Jeep.

"You'll never even be able to lift it out."

"I thought I might sort of roll it into place."

He studied me for a moment.

"Go on up to the graveyard," he said. "I'll send someone along to help you. Don't stop on the way. Once the stone is set, you'll have to leave immediately. I'm afraid I can't offer you any hospitality this evening."

"I didn't expect any. I didn't even expect help."

He nodded and got out.

I think he meant it, I think he was going to let me go. But while we were talking, the two trucks had made it to the space in front of the garage, dwarfing the pickup parked there. They'd evidently had to take it easy coming down the slope, low gear.

I didn't recognize the two men getting out of the first truck, or the driver of the second truck. But I knew the man who swung himself awkwardly down from the passenger's side of the second truck. I knew him despite the thinning hair and the thickening waist, despite what appeared to be a prosthetic device instead of a right hand.

He was my father. Danny O'Neal.

Chapter

13

I HAVE BEEN driving cars since I was fifteen. I learned to drive on my mother's Oldsmobile, which had an automatic transmission, power steering, and all kinds of other options, but my first car was a used Ford Escort that had nothing added, and I've used a stick shift ever since. I hadn't stalled a car in as long as I could remember. Until I saw my father getting out of that truck just as I was starting to drive away. My foot slipped off the clutch and the Jeep died.

Jared Farrell froze on the step.

Danny sort of hung from the cab of the truck.

I got out of the Jeep and walked over to him.

"I guess the marker for your grave was a little premature," I said.

"Freddie," he said. He looked puzzled, as if he couldn't figure out what else to say. I studied his face.

Sam had warned me that Danny hadn't aged well, and I had tried to prepare myself. But I was still stricken by the sight of him.

His face was weak and puffy, with hanging jowls, and his skin had a pasty white look that meant he hadn't eaten right in a long time. The thinning hair that sprung from the top of his head was gray, and there was no more red in his sideburns. I knew his eyes used to be hazel, like mine, but now they were so watery the color had been washed out. He looked away. I didn't blame him. Seeing him, I could understand why Jared Farrell had found it hard to believe he was my father. I kept staring, searching for some sign of the handsome, laughing man of the old photographs. Not there.

He let go of the truck frame, dropping his left arm to his side. His right one still hung limply, a stiff, rubbery imitation of a hand protruding from the sleeve of his work shirt.

"What happened to your hand?" I asked.

"It's a long story," he said.

I waited, but he didn't say anything more.

"You might as well come in, Miss O'Neal." Farrell's voice startled me. I had forgotten he was there. "It seems I'll be offering you hospitality after all." He looked past me to Danny and added, "We can all talk inside."

The three other men from the convoy had melted away somewhere. Still not looking at me, Danny walked up the steps and into the house. As soon as I was certain I could walk without shaking, I followed.

Jackie Ellis was the only person in the living room. She was sort of half reclining on the couch, blond hair straggling onto a rumpled tank top, and her blue eyes had the same unfocused look they had the first time I met her.

"Where did he go?" I asked.

"He'll be back," she said. "This has upset him, too, you know. He didn't want you to see him."

"Yeah. I guess not."

"Why don't you sit? Jared will be in soon, once he's seen to the stuff in the trucks."

I perched on the edge of one of the chairs.

"Can I get you anything?" she asked.

"No."

"I'm sorry," she said.

"You told me that before, but you wouldn't tell me what you were sorry about."

"I'm sorry I couldn't tell you the truth. I'm sorry I helped make you believe Danny was dead."

"Anything else?"

"I'm not sure. I have to think about it."

I waited. But thinking about it was evidently going to take some time.

"Maybe you could go get Danny while you're thinking," I said.

She shook her head. "He'll be back."

"Well, tell me something!" I said it too sharply, I had to control my voice. "Tell me what you're doing here."

"Taking care of Jared. I take care of Jared. And Jared takes care of me."

"Can you leave if you want to?"

"The deal is that I don't leave."

"That doesn't sound like a very good deal to me."

"Maybe it will. Later on this evening, you might like it better."

There wasn't any real threat in her words, not even in her voice. But it chilled me.

"You think Jared won't want me to leave after I've talked to Danny?"

She nodded slowly.

"But he won't want to kill you, either. Jared's old-fashioned that way—he doesn't like to kill women. He's chivalrous, really. Some men don't mind killing women, because they don't have respect for them to start with. But Jared isn't like that. He killed a woman once, but it was in a blind rage, and he felt bad about it, he told me that. I'd guess he'll ask you to stay on here."

The realization of what woman Jared Farrell had killed

dawned on me slowly, spreading from my toes up to my stomach, taking the blood away from my vital organs, and then exploding in my head.

"Oh, hell. He did it. Jared Farrell blew his own son away and then shot the hooker, too. That's it, isn't it?"

I slumped in the chair without waiting for her to answer. She regarded me solemnly.

"See what I mean? Leaving or living. Not much of a choice, is it?"

"I'll find out if I have to make it."

"It's not bad here. There's not much to do, but I get whatever I want to eat and drink, as long as I plan ahead so someone can bring it in, and as long as I fix it. Jared won't let the men near me, but that's okay."

"You miss it," I said, startled enough that for a moment I was paying attention to her, not to my own problems. "You miss turning tricks."

"Sometimes I do." She shut her eyes for a moment, trying to clear them. "Sometimes I felt a rush, a sense of control over the poor suckers who were paying me to make them feel good. I miss that. It was the only time I ever felt in control, and I miss feeling in control of something. I don't miss the scary ones, or the ones I couldn't face unless I was drunk. I don't miss them." She paused, then added, "I miss my dance classes most of all."

"Why didn't you go to the cops?"

"Oh, God." She reached for a wineglass that was sitting on the coffee table. I hadn't noticed it earlier. "How could I trust the cops?"

"You're right, you couldn't. No more than Danny could. Cops don't trust people on the edge, and people on the edge can't trust them. What about running? Why didn't you go someplace else and start over?"

"Danny tried that, and he didn't make it. What makes you think I could?"

"Some people are tougher than others."

"You're like your mom, aren't you? Danny told me about your mom, how tough she is. Uncompromising, that was his word. He said a little about you, too." That came out apologetically, as an afterthought.

I couldn't ask any more questions, because I was beginning to hurt too much to think about anyone but myself. And then the conversation was really over, because Danny came into the room. His face wasn't as pasty, it was flushed and puffier. He looked as if he had downed a couple of quick ones in the kitchen, something stronger than Jackie's white wine.

"Freddie," he said again, still puzzled. He glanced at me, and then tried to find something interesting somewhere else in the room. "Yes, Freddie. I heard you were looking for me."

He sat in the chair across from me and buried his face in his remaining hand.

"I think I should leave," Jackie said, struggling to sit up.

"No, please don't," Danny begged.

"It's okay, Jackie," I said. "I don't think we have anything private to say to each other."

That must have made sense to her. She dropped back onto the couch. I stared at Danny, he didn't look at me. We didn't have much public to say, either.

"You think I should have called, don't you?" he asked when the silence must have gotten too much for him.

"I used to think that, yeah. I used to think you should have called to let me know where you were, let me know you were all right. I used to think that you didn't call because you didn't care. For a lot of years I thought that. But I guess it was more complicated, wasn't it?"

"I thought about you." It was almost a whisper. "I swear I thought about you."

"Sure you did, Danny. You thought about me. You thought about Mom, too. Jackie told me you did."

He started to cry. He didn't lift his face out of his hand, but I knew. He started to cry. I wanted to care, I really tried to care. All those years I thought about seeing him again, I thought I was going to care when I finally sat across from him. I didn't move.

"Maybe you could tell me about it," I said. "Maybe you could tell me why you never called."

He just sat there and cried.

"Okay. Let's start with something easier. How did you know Jared Farrell shot his son?" Easier for me if I didn't think of the crying man as my father.

"I saw him." He kept his face down, his hand still over his eyes, but I could hear. "I had heard a rumor that the place where I was working, the auto repair shop, was going to close. I wanted to go back to bartending, and I thought Tommy might hire me back. I had left the Bunkhouse over something minor, really a misunderstanding—Tommy thought I was taking kickbacks from a couple of the girls—and I wanted to talk with him, work it out. I got there just in time to see Jared walk out with a shotgun in his hands."

The auto repair shop. The chop shop, Farrell had called it.

"I understand why you didn't go to the police. But why didn't you try to cut a deal with Jared?"

"You mean blackmail him?"

I hadn't thought I meant that at all.

"I was thinking more like keeping quiet in exchange for a job," I said.

Danny lifted his head and glanced at me, but he couldn't hold eye contact.

"Jared would have seen it as blackmail. He never would have trusted me. And he might have killed me, blown me away just like he did his own son. I didn't want to take the chance. I decided I'd be better off on the road somewhere."

"Where'd you get the money to leave?"

"The garage where I worked. I cleaned out the safe before I left. I knew they wouldn't report it."

This was getting worse and worse. Suddenly he pushed himself up out of the chair, using his fake hand for leverage.

"I'll be back in a minute," he said.

"Why don't you just bring the bottle in here?" I snapped it out the same way Mom would have.

Danny stopped on the spot and reeled for a moment, as if he almost didn't know who had said it. I felt my face turning red, but I didn't take it back.

"I'll do that," he said. He didn't look at me as he left the room.

"You don't have to be so tough on him," Jackie said quietly.

"What the hell do you know?" I still sounded like Mom. "I'm sorry." That sounded more like me.

"He's hurting, having to face you. I can see it. And I guess you have a right to be angry at him. But how can you yell at a crying drunk?"

A tear rolled onto her nose. She brushed it away. I didn't yell at her.

We were still sitting quietly when Danny came back with a half-full pint of Bushmills and a glass in his hand.

"I should have asked if you wanted anything," he said.

"That's okay," I told him.

"I need a refill," Jackie said. "I'll get you a beer."

She got up carefully and walked through the archway. I didn't tell her not to bring the beer.

"Where were we?" he asked.

"You had just burglarized the chop shop," I said.

He took a gulp of Bushmills, out of the bottle, then poured more into the glass. If I'd taken a gulp like that, it would have come out my ears.

"Why do you want to hear this?" he asked.

"Part of me doesn't want to hear it," I said. "But I guess I have to. I guess it's all so far away from what I wanted it to be, from what I thought it was, that I have to."

He nodded. "What else do you want to know?"

"What you did all those years."

"I went to Mexico, because I thought the money would last longer down there. The food made me sick and I got tired of nobody to talk to, so I came back." He paused for a gulp from the glass. "I didn't stay anyplace very long. When the money ran out, I joined the 'bos. A lot of years just slipped away."

He stared past me, as if trying to see where they went.

"Do you have any good memories?" Nothing I could say would make him feel better. I hoped he could cheer himself a little.

"I don't know. Not many." He struggled to come up with one, as if he had a sudden atavistic impulse to give me what I had asked him for. "Dawn in New Orleans, the French Quarter, lining up with the truck drivers to get coffee from a spigot in a wall. Really. A whole wall with spigots of coffee."

There was something pathetic about that as the only good memory he could come up with. Even I could have done better.

"Why'd you come back?"

"I woke up one morning in an alley and I wanted to come home."

That was probably the only thing I had been right about, that sooner or later Danny O'Neal would want to come back to Nevada. He just never made it all the way to Reno. I looked at him, thinking of all the crooked trails he had walked in his life.

"You haven't told me how you lost your hand," I said.

"Ah. Yes. We're coming to that. See, the only way I could live in Nevada was to make my peace with Jared Farrell, I knew that. And he gave me a job—what you said I should have done to begin with, I finally did. I went to work for Jared. I slept in a bed at night, shaved every morning, put on clean clothes, and went to work, for the first time in years. And that was when I met Jackie. She's a sweet girl, and I wanted to show her a good time, so I started skimming just a little out of the register, just enough to buy her things. Jared found out. And that's what happened to my hand."

He hid his head again, but not before I saw the tears.

"Oh, God," I said, working to control the flip-flops in my stomach. "Farrell cut it off. He decided not to kill you, just to make an example of you."

"Do you think I should apologize, Miss O'Neal?"

I hadn't heard Farrell come in, and his voice startled me. He was standing just inside the front door.

"Not really," I said. "It makes sense, doesn't it?"

"I thought you might see it that way."

"Jared. Oh, good, you're back." Jackie stepped in from the archway and handed me a beer without looking at me. But I could see the streak on the side of her face where the tears had smeared her mascara. She placed her wineglass on the coffee table. "What can I get you?"

"I'll join Miss O'Neal in a beer," he said.

She turned and left again without comment.

He was an imposing figure, Jared Farrell, standing there. Probably seemed even more so in comparison with the two crying drunks I'd been talking to. He was so old and thin and dried out that he was almost mummified. But his eyes were clear.

"I'd appreciate it if you'd tell me the rest of it, sir," I said. "First, the grave. You took me to Danny's grave."

"I wanted to make sure he understood. I had him dig it, and then while he was standing in it, I gave him a choice. His life or his hand. When he chose his life, I left the grave there, so he would remember. I'm afraid I didn't consult him about the marker."

I looked at Danny, hoping he would say something, but he didn't. He had almost finished the Bushmills, and he sat there swirling the little bit left in the glass. I couldn't help wishing he had made the other choice, and I hated myself for wishing it.

"And one more thing," I said, turning back to Farrell. "Why did you shoot your son?"

"Because he was weak and stupid and I couldn't stand him any longer," Farrell said. "That's why."

"There must have been more to it than that," I said. "If people got shot for being weak and stupid, we'd all be vulnerable."

"But his weakness and stupidity left me vulnerable. The purpose of the bars—the reason I own them—is so that no one will wonder what I do for a living, no one will pry into my life. I told Tommy to get rid of the girls, or if he had to have them, to move to a county where they were legal. Illegal girls attract illegal drugs and other problems. I didn't want them around. He wouldn't do what I told him to do."

"He was weak, stupid, and wouldn't follow your orders. No choice there. Okay. What about the girl?" I asked.

"I didn't intend to shoot the girl. She screamed, and I was so mad at Tommy that I fired again. But she came from a good family, and I think her parents, when they thought about it, were grateful for what I did."

"Yeah, probably. After all, she was weak, stupid, and didn't follow their orders. Might as well shoot her, too."

"I hear an edge in your voice, Miss O'Neal. I'm surprised that you would defend the weak and the stupid."

"I'm just defending those who don't follow orders."

Jackie slipped in and handed Farrell his beer. She placed a new pint of Bushmills on the coffee table.

"Do you want anything else?" she whispered.

Farrell waved her away. She made her way to the couch bent over, to stay under his line of vision.

Danny refilled his glass.

"But why shoot Gary Hanrahan?" I asked.

"Danny saw me leave that day. The relief bartender saw me arrive. Gary Hanrahan. I promised him drinking money for the rest of his life, and he promised silence. He was trustworthy for years. When you started asking questions, he called, saying he thought you ought to know about Danny. I told Cliff to make sure he stayed quiet."

"Cliff, your other son. The one still alive. The one who follows orders."

I got one of those you're-lucky-you're-a-woman looks from Farrell. He'd been building up to it, and I'd been expecting him to say it.

"I'm certain that over time, as we get to know each other better, you will learn the wisdom of following my orders."

Farrell had been standing all this time, looking down at the three of us. I had to stand up to face him.

"Thanks for the offer, sir, but I don't think I want to stay."

"I didn't offer you a choice. Jackie will show you to your room. I had it prepared when I heard you were coming, just in case you had to stay. I'm looking forward to your companionship. It will be a pleasure, talking to someone sober."

I sat back down. Goddamn Sam. He had said Farrell might not want me to leave.

"People will miss me," I said. "People know I was coming here."

"And they will find the remains of your Jeep. Far from here. After a few days they will stop looking for your body. If anyone calls me, I'll tell them how sorry I am you didn't get here."

I knew without asking that the Jeep wasn't out front any longer. One more thing Farrell took care of, besides the trucks.

"But that's going to call attention to you. Enough kidnaps, enough murders, all tied to you—don't you think more and more people are going to ask questions?"

"I hope not. On the other hand, if it takes them long enough to get around to it, I'll be dead and it won't matter."

"Are you ill?" I asked, trying not to sound hopeful.

"No. Just old." A smile twitched his face, and I caught a glimpse of the death's head beneath the skin. "And you'll appreciate the irony, I know, that I have lived long enough to see a Marine colonel make gunrunning respectable, and my son didn't."

"Yeah. Too bad about that," I said.

Jackie's glass was empty, and she tried to slide off the couch and get to the archway under Farrell's line of vision, but she didn't make it.

"There will be eight of us for dinner, Jackie. As long as you're in the kitchen, you might get it started," Farrell said. "Since this is your first night with us, Miss O'Neal, you may consider yourself a guest. Starting tomorrow, you'll help Jackie."

"I'm afraid you'll be disappointed. I never learned to cook." I glanced at Danny as I said it, but I couldn't tell whether it registered, whether he remembered fighting with Mom over food.

"You'll learn now," Farrell said.

I had my mouth open to answer when the other three men from the trucks walked in. Farrell was still so close to the front door that they had to kind of slide past him, but no one asked him to move. He introduced them as Bob, Larry, and Ed. I wasn't sure which was which. Two were tall, thirtyish, with military brush-cut hair, wearing work shirts and jeans. The third was short and heavy, twentyish, with military brush-cut hair, wearing a work shirt and jeans. I think he was Bob. Either Larry or Ed went to get beer.

"If you'll excuse us," Farrell said, "those of us with two hands are going to shoot a little pool before dinner."

"Fine," I answered. "I think I'll find my room."

Danny didn't look up when I left.

The kitchen was at the end of the hall, the back of the house. Ed or Larry nodded as he passed me with the beers on his way back to the living room. The size of the kitchen, the space, harked back to a time when cooking from scratch for a bunch of people for dinner was the rule. The old stove was big enough for a hotel, and the oven looked like it could handle a thirty-pound turkey. Jackie seemed tiny, tearing a head of iceberg lettuce into a bowl, in the far corner near the double sink.

"I don't have to be a guest," I said, "if there's something I can do to help."

"Not really." She stopped tearing lettuce to take a sip of wine. "I'm fixing a salad, but other than that it's just going to be steak and chili and bread. We get those big cans of chili, the kind restaurants buy, and I can manage to turn the steaks on the broiler." She also managed a laugh.

"Okay, if you're sure. Farrell said I had a room. Where is it?"

She gestured toward the kitchen door, the way I had come in. "The stairs. Up the stairs, first door on the left. The bathroom is next to it."

It wasn't much of a room. It had a bed and a dresser, both old. Somebody had placed my flight bag—the one that had been in the Jeep—on the dresser and hung a robe in the closet. Getting the room ready probably just meant putting sheets on the bed. And maybe there was an extra towel in the bathroom.

I had a great view of the sunset out the window. I had planned to set the stone and say good-bye to Danny with that sunset and be out of there. So much for plans.

I stared at the mountains to the west until I heard Jackie calling up the stairs that dinner was ready.

We sat, the eight of us, including the young man who had been guarding the gate, at a mahogany table under a crystal chandelier in a formal dining room. The food was served family style, the steaks on a platter and the chili in a tureen. Danny and Jackie were both too drunk to eat. I don't know how she got the food on the table.

Farrell acted as head of the family, and the men were obviously making an effort at table manners. I had a sense that was one of his orders. The conversation was pretty much the polite sort about passing the salt and pepper. Nobody paid attention to Jackie playing with her food or Danny ignoring his. I tuned out, until I realized that the topic of conversation had changed. Farrell and the three men were talking about the cargo on the trucks and a plane that was coming in to pick it up the next day.

That was when I remembered the airstrip and the Navion. The Navion was going to have to be my ticket out of there.

"Doesn't look like Jackie wants any coffee," I said when the plates had been pushed back. "I guess I could make it."

Farrell raised his eyebrows. "Thank you, Miss O'Neal. I appreciate your spirit."

I was hoping there would be both regular and decaf, so that I could make two pots, a charge of caffeine for me and none for them, but there was only regular. While I was starting the automatic coffeemaker, the young guard came into the kitchen. He nodded at me and then began putting together two dinners to go.

"Can I help you?" I asked.

"No. I'll take them, but thanks." He avoided my eyes, and I didn't try to find out any more. Two guards out there somewhere.

He took the two plates out a back door. There was a dead bolt on it, but not the kind that required a key from the inside. I would be able to get out that door.

My ineptness in the kitchen turned out to be a plus. Automatic coffeemaker or not, none of the men drank more than half a cup, the coffee was so lousy. I drank two. I figured the caffeine and nervous tension would keep me awake until dawn. I also washed the dishes, to keep myself out of everybody's way. I left them draining. Drying them and putting them away might have aroused suspicion. Enough was enough.

When I checked the living room, Farrell was shooting pool again with his two-handed buddies. I had forgotten to ask him what happened to his missing fingers, and now I hoped I would never know. Danny and Jackie were nowhere to be seen. I thought about that. Maybe Farrell didn't bother keeping Danny away from her. If they got some comfort from each other, it was all right with me.

I poked around in my feelings, the embers of a fifteen-year-old flame, but I didn't care if I said good-bye to him. At some point, seeing the fake grave or getting the stone, I don't know just when, but at some point I had already said good-bye. Nothing I had seen in the living room changed that.

I went up to the room that held my flight bag and lay down on the bed. The house was too well built—I couldn't hear the crack of cue on ball. I went back to the stairs and positioned myself so that I could listen. I wanted to know when they quit and went to bed.

I was still going to have to worry about the two guards. The first one would be at the front gate. I wasn't certain where the second one would be. Maybe near the airstrip, maybe not. I would have to take my chances.

I rested my head on my knees and shut my eyes, so that I could hear better. Still, I had to scramble to get back to my room when I finally heard someone starting up the stairs.

They passed down the hall in a group. But counting them wouldn't have helped anyway, because I didn't know how many of them slept in the house. I stood against the wall of the bedroom, listening to doors opening and shutting, water running, toilets flushing. I was certain it was after midnight by the time everyone settled down.

My escape was going to have to wait until almost dawn for two reasons. The first was that Farrell was so old, the odds were he didn't sleep much. Just before dawn felt like the best time for him to be in a deep sleep, whether it was scientifically valid or not. It felt like the best time for all of them to be asleep.

But the second reason was more important anyway. There was no moon. Without a moon, I couldn't see well enough to steal the airplane. I had to wait until dawn.

Pulling an all-nighter gives one time enough to think about a lot of things, including whether it might not be wiser to stay for another day or so, find out where the other guard was stationed, maybe even wait for a full moon. But I couldn't do it. Thinking about staying there was like thinking about being buried alive. I got panicky when my mind even brushed against it. Besides, I was certain Farrell wouldn't expect me to make a run for it so quickly. If I stayed, even another day, I might give it away that I was plotting my escape.

I kept imagining traces of gray in the sky, fading stars, and I wished I had been assigned a room on the east side of the house. I paced the floor as quietly as I could, afraid to lie down for very long, certain my nerves would never let me sleep, but not willing to chance it.

Finally, the gray was real. I waited a few minutes just to make sure. But there was even a touch of color on the mountaintops where the first glow of the sun was approaching. I hung my flight bag over my shoulder, opened the door, checked the hall, and slipped to the stairs.

I hadn't noticed any squeaks coming up, but I still tested the treads, one at a time, before putting full weight on them. I tested each step down the hall, too, taking my time to reach the kitchen. Not enough light came in for me to see clearly. I had to feel my way to the door, remembering where the tile counters were, the cupboards, remembering the wall, moving my hand carefully so that even if it encountered an unexpected plate or cup, nothing would clatter.

I touched the door. I felt for the dead bolt, turned it slowly until the click echoed like a gunshot in my skull, turned the handle, and I was outside. I leaned against the side of the house to breathe the cool, fresh air, feeling the rough stucco through my denim jacket, waiting for my eyes to grow accustomed to the partial light.

The back porch was narrow and made of wood. I could make out the steps and the railing. From that point, I would have to hurry, cross the yard at a fast lope so that I reached the far buildings with breath to spare before there was enough light for me to be easily visible.

It couldn't have taken more than a few seconds, but I felt as if I had been exposed for an hour by the time I reached the shadow of the old barns. Inside one of them were two trucks filled with high-tech guns and ammunition headed for the Mideast. Marine colonels or no, I didn't think much of gunrunners. What Farrell was doing was partly legal, partly not—I got that much from the dinner-table conversation—depending on which merchandise went to which recipient and what American public policy was at the moment. If I'd stayed, I'd have wanted to blow up a truck just for spite.

But it wasn't worth getting killed for.

I skirted the barns and headed for the airstrip, again at a lope. The sky was bright enough that I could see the Navion clearly. It was painted to look like an Army plane, and in fact a lot of them had been used by the military during World War II and Korea. General MacArthur had flown one. A couple of thousand were made for civilian use before they quit manufacturing them altogether in the early fifties. Navions had become classics for private plane buffs, and a number of them had been rebuilt and restored. I had to hope that this was one of them.

A walkaround wasn't going to do me much good, because I couldn't fix anything, but I did one anyway. There was fuel in the tanks, no water in the fuel drains, the propeller worked, and the paint job was new enough that I had to hope somebody was maintaining the engine. I was checking the tires, thinking about how high off the ground the plane was, how much bigger the landing gear was than the Cherokee's, when I spotted a dark streak. The hydraulic system was leaking. That meant trouble retracting the landing gear, and I had to get the gear up to get the plane over the mountains. Down, the gear would create too much drag.

Forewarned is forearmed. I would have to pump up the

hydraulic system by hand. I disconnected the tie-downs, pulled myself up on the wing, slid the canopy back, and climbed in.

The one real break I had to hope for was that either the plane didn't need an ignition key or that it was kept with the plane. Planes aren't like cars—casual thieves don't take them—and some pilots think it makes sense to leave the key where you're going to use it. Particularly in a situation like this, where the compound is guarded. But I didn't have to look for one. This plane had a master switch instead.

I closed the canopy, belted myself in, checked the gauges, and flipped the switch.

"Come on, God!" I whispered.

The engine caught and the propeller whirred. I gave it a little fuel, released the brake, and the plane started moving toward the mountains to the north. The noise was loud enough to wake the angels. I was only going to have one chance at this. I pressed the left rudder. The plane turned slowly, lining up with the runway, facing west.

Just as I opened the throttle, a man came running out about five hundred feet in front of me, with something too big to be a hunting rifle in his hands. He dropped to his knee and aimed.

I decided I was dead one way or the other. I headed the plane straight at him, picking up speed. He didn't move.

Neither of us heard the Harley over the airplane roar, and then it was right on top of him. Sam must have come out of the mountains to the north. He crossed the runway with the heavy saddlebags in his hand, and he slammed the man in the side of the head with them, almost losing his bike in the process. The man fell over, dropping the rifle, struggling to disentangle himself from the saddlebags. Sam grabbed the rifle and took a wide swing around the plane, coming up on the passenger side.

I really thought for a minute I was going to keep going.
I wasn't sure how he got there, and not certain I could trust
him. But I braked. I reached up and slid back the canopy just
as Sam jumped from the Harley to the wing.

"Lord, I am too old and too fat for this," he yelled as he
climbed in. He slipped the rifle between his knees, settled
into the passenger seat, and snapped his seat belt.

"The only reason I stopped for you is that the hydraulic
system isn't working," I told him. I closed the canopy again.
"You're going to have to pump if we're going to get out of
this valley." I pointed at the handle, which was hidden under
the instrument panel, between the two seats.

I ran the engine up full, still holding on to the brake. I
wanted fifty knots at liftoff, almost stall speed. I released the
brake and felt the power surge through the yoke into my
hands. The runway was short, and I had to keep the nose up,
keep the propeller out of the dirt. I let it fly at the end of the
runway, lowered the nose, and inched the flaps up, knowing
I'd need the hydraulic system to get them back down.

"Pump!" I yelled at Sam.

He worked the handle like crazy. The landing gear came
up slowly, awkwardly. The plane careened along, barely
above the level of the sagebrush. Every grain of sand
seemed a rock, every rock a boulder. The mountain was
looming, and we weren't going to get over it.

I sucked the nose up, stomped the rudder, and let the
plane slide onto its side. We were going to have to make a
circle inside the valley to pick up altitude.

"Jesus!" Sam yelled as we banked.

"Shut up and hold on!" I yelled back.

Slowly the plane came around.

The guard came running out of the hut at the south end of
the compound. He stared up at us, not knowing if we were
supposed to be there or not. I held the plane at a fifteen-

degree angle as we turned east, gaining speed and altitude.
I could see figures streaming out of the house, none of them
armed. But by the time we were heading back to the north
end of the valley, over the airstrip, a second man was
standing beside the one Sam had hit. He had another of the
big rifles and was taking aim.

Sam picked up the rifle again. I reached up and slid back
the canopy. Sam didn't bother to aim. He just opened fire.
Both men started running. I had to bank left to get us
heading west, but by then we were going to be out of range.

This time we cleared the mountain.

Sam closed the canopy and settled back into his seat. The
plane flies just fine with it open, but the noise is worse.

I took the plane in a wide swing over Death Valley, and
then banked right to take us north.

"I guess I can breathe now," Sam shouted over the
engine, still loud even with the canopy closed. When I
didn't comment he added, "I sure am going to miss that
bike."

"You didn't need to do that," I said. "You didn't need to
dump the bike. I might have made it without you."

"And you might not, too."

I glanced at him. "And I might have been in less trouble
if you hadn't told Farrell I was coming."

"Oh, hell, Freddie. Are we back to that? I didn't tell him
the first time, and I didn't tell him this time, either."

"Then how did he know? And what are you doing here?"

"As to what I'm doing here, after that last little scene on
your porch, I knew you weren't about to let me come here
with you. So I decided the thing to do was ride to Beatty,
check into a motel, and pay the gas station attendant to keep
an eye out for the Jeep. He told me when you stopped for
gas. I didn't want to alert Farrell I was here, so I circled
around and came up on the compound the back way,

through the mountains by the graveyard. I just camped up there and waited. It's a good thing I woke up before dawn. I didn't think you'd run for it that quickly."

"They don't have a guard up there?"

"Nope. They figured nobody'd come that way. And only an old biker would know about it. As to how Farrell knew, you must have told someone else about your plan to put a stone on the grave."

I went back over the last couple of weeks to think who I'd told. Deke. Mom. And Hardy McCullen, who had helped me lift the stone. Cliff Farrell's bartender.

"You're right. I did. And I'm sorry. I'm sorry about your bike, too. Was it insured?"

Sam laughed. "Hell, no. Not insured, not registered. I don't even have a driver's license."

I remembered then that I hadn't been able to find him through the DMV. I considered saying something about responsibility, but it wasn't worth shouting over the engine.

The sunrise over the eastern desert was pure pink for one minute and then a blinding gold the next. The few stratocumulus clouds looked as if they had caught fire.

"Where are we going?" Sam asked.

"Reno. I want to go home."

"You want company?"

"I don't know, Sam. I'm glad you were there—you're right, I might not have made it without you—but you have too many surprises. I'm just not comfortable with you."

"I'll give you another one. I didn't sleep with your mother."

I involuntarily jerked the yoke. The nose came up, and I had to correct before we stalled.

"Why not?"

"Well, we talked about it at the time, but it just didn't

seem like a good idea. Besides, Ramona isn't really my type. Now. Where are we going?"

"Let me think about it," I said. "We've got a couple of hours before we reach Reno. Let me think about it."

The long shadows across the desert burned away to red and brown and chalk-white as the sun hit the center of the sky. To the west, the dark Sierras sprouted black trees. We rode together in silence until the grid of buildings, the spikes of Bally's and the MGM Grand sticking up out of the desert, signaled the city.

I picked up the microphone to call Reno Clearance Control.

Chapter 14

CANNON INTERNATIONAL SECURITY guards weren't happy with the story of how I happened to have that plane. Jerry McIntire came over from the charter terminal to vouch for my character, but all the good that came from it was a couple of cups of coffee, one for Sam and one for me, while we all sat back and waited for Officer Maddox. He wasn't on duty that early in the day, but I insisted somebody call him at home, and he agreed to come to the airport.

He believed us.

"Cliff Farrell was a suspect early on," Maddox said. He had taken the time to put on his uniform, and the security guards backed off when he got there. "We knew he had been gone from the bar for about half an hour earlier in the evening. But he told us that the icemaker wasn't working right, and he had to bring some in, and that part of it was true. We just couldn't tie him to the murder."

"You think you can do it now?" I asked.

"I think it's going to be a mess, trying to straighten this all out. I'll try to get warrants to pick up both Farrells, although bringing Cliff in for questioning may be the best we can do, since all we have is hearsay. And we'll see what Jared does next. He hasn't reported the airplane stolen. If he had, I'd have to take both of you in. You'd probably be safer in jail for the next few days anyway."

"I want to go home, Maddox. I promise not to go anywhere else without telling you."

He sighed. "Come on. I'll give you a ride. What about you, Courter?" he asked Sam.

"It's okay," I said before Sam had a chance to answer. "He's coming with me."

Butch and Sundance were waiting on the front porch when Maddox dropped Sam and me off. They scattered when they realized that Sam was coming in. I had been gone less than twenty-four hours, I had left plenty of food, and I hoped there wouldn't be any half-eaten surprises.

I was lucky. No feathers, no tails, no claws on the office floor.

"Ramona is sure going to be glad I'm here to look after you," Sam said as we both settled heavily on the sofa in what passes for my living room.

"Oh, God," I groaned. "Why did you say that? I have to call her. I have to tell her Danny isn't dead after all."

"Maybe not. My hunch is that if you wait a few days, you won't have to make that call."

"You think Jared will kill him," I said.

Sam nodded. "I think so. He has to bet you'll talk, and a couple of deputies will come calling. Without either Danny O'Neal or Gary Hanrahan, there's no way of convicting him of killing his son."

I knew he was right, and again I tried to care about Danny, but I just couldn't summon up any feeling for the dissipated coward I had met in the compound. At the same moment, I realized I was exhausted.

"Sam, I have to go to bed. Alone."

"I'll sleep here on the couch," he said. "I think it'd be best if anything between us was kept on ice for a while anyway.

If you get involved with me now, you'll always wonder why."

He was right one more time.

Over the next few days, I kept expecting him to leave, but he never got around to it. At night, he'd stretch out on the couch.

When Maddox picked Cliff Farrell up for questioning, he took a look around the house and discovered there was an empty space in the gun case in Farrell's den where a rifle used to be. The state decided to try the case, even on what was circumstantial evidence, and Farrell eventually plea-bargained guilty to voluntary manslaughter, no jail time. I thought voluntary manslaughter was supposed to be a crime of passion, but maybe this was. After all, he was protecting his father.

There was no trace of either Danny O'Neal or Jackie Ellis when the state police drove out to Bullfrog, not even the wooden cross in the graveyard. Jared Farrell said I was a crazy women who had wrecked her Jeep and then gone joyriding in his classic Navion, but he wasn't even going to press charges, since he got it back with no damage done. Unfortunately, my Jeep hadn't fared so well. Farrell turned the remains of it over to the police, who turned it over to my insurance company, who called it a total loss.

But I could stand the loss of the Jeep. If Farrell had pressed charges and I had been convicted of a felony, I would have lost my PI license. I was never really certain why he didn't try to collect my scalp. I might have tried to collect his, but I decided he was too old, he might die before he even got to trial. Better to cut my losses.

Al won election to the state legislature, and he and Mom renewed their wedding vows. I didn't go this time, either.

Mom paid me, just like a real client, or even better. I never did tell her I found Danny alive. I didn't want to go through it all again, and I figured Sam was right that I didn't have to. Odds were good that she was a widow, whenever and however it happened. I would have liked to talk to her about Sam, but I couldn't do it over the phone, and I didn't see her before she and Al left on their vacation.

Maudie Hanrahan bought me lunch one day, to thank me for my efforts on her father's behalf. But we didn't have anything in common except for dead fathers, and I never saw her again.

Sam stayed, sleeping on the couch, until we heard Farrell wasn't pressing charges. His Harley was gone, my Jeep was gone, so we mostly hung out and watched movies. We went to the Mother Lode once for dinner, but Deke acted weird, so we switched to Harrah's.

Then I walked into the living room one morning and found him with his jacket on, staring out the window.

"What?" I asked.

"I can't take it any longer," he said. "I can't sleep on this couch another night. I'm thinking about going back to Vegas."

"Oh." Part of me wanted to tell him that I was just getting used to him being around, that Butch and Sundance were just getting past the spooked stage, and maybe he didn't have to leave yet. But I said "Oh." After a pause I added, "For how long?"

"I don't know." He still wasn't looking at me. "I'll have to get a job, save up money for a new bike."

"You could do that in Reno." It came out as a blurt before I could stop it.

This time he looked at me. "I'm too old and I'm too fat and I think I ought to leave now."

"Sam, I'm sorry." I tried not to cry, but I couldn't help it. I started to sob. "I'm really sorry."

"Ah, Freddie, so am I."

He held me for a long time, even after I stopped crying. Then we walked to the Mother Lode for breakfast, and I went with him to the bus station. He held me until the bus for Vegas was ready to leave.

"Maybe I could fly down to see you," I said.

"Maybe so," he answered.

I thought of facing Moira and Doc, and I knew it wasn't likely that I'd do it.

"I'll call you," he said, and I started to cry again.

He kissed me once and then he was on the bus.

I must have stood watching the street until the bus was halfway to Fallon. I walked home, and for the first time since I'd lived there, the house seemed empty to me.

I picked up the phone. If I hurried, I could beat the bus, meet him at the station.

"Hey, Jerry," I said. "I need to charter the Cherokee. I'm flying to Las Vegas this afternoon."